Public Library

D0287137

The next day, Jesse went to Mike's house.

They played video games and ate pizza. Around 3 p.m., Mike's dad drove him home. He had to read three chapters of a novel for Language Arts and study for an American history test.

"Hey, Dad, I'm home," he called, slamming the door behind him.

Big Bob was sitting in the living room with Jesse's dad. Neither man looked happy.

Mark Alvarez stood and came toward his son.

"Jesse, did you go out to the reservation to see Aaron yesterday?"

Jesse nodded. "Yesterday morning. I rode my bike."

"His father came to see me today," Big Bob told him. "Aaron's missing."

WITHDRAWN

Baldwinsville Public Library
33 East Genesee Street
Baldwinsville, NY 13027-2575

DREAMCATCHER

A Novel By

ANN CURTIN

Zumaya Thresholds   *Austin TX*

2015

This book is a work of fiction. Names, characters, places and incidents are products of the author's imagination or are used fictitiously. Any resemblance to actual persons or events is purely coincidental.

DREAMCATCHER
© 2015 By Ann Curtin
ISBN 978-1-61271-246-8
Cover Art © Eva Montealegre
Cover Design © Tamian Wood

All rights reserved. Except for use in review, the reproduction or utilization of this work in whole or in part in any form by any electronic, mechanical or other means now known or hereafter invented, is prohibited without the written permission of the author or publisher.

"Zumaya Thresholds" and the dodo colophon are trademarks of Zumaya Publications LLC, Austin TX.

Library of Congress Cataloging-in-Publication Data

Curtin, Ann, 1958- author.
 Dreamcatcher / Ann Curtin.
    pages cm
   ISBN 978-1-61271-246-8 (print-trade pbk. : alk. paper) -- ISBN 978-1-61271-247-5 (electronic-multiple formats) -- ISBN 978-1-61271-248-2 (electronic-epub)
[1. Ranch life--Wyoming--Fiction. 2. Middle schools--Fiction. 3. Schools--Fiction. 4. Single-parent families--Fiction. 5. Ghosts--Fiction. 6. Friendship--Fiction. 7. Bullying--Fiction. 8. Indians of North America--Wyoming--Fiction. 9. Wyoming--Fiction.] I. Title.
 PZ7.1.C867Dre 2015
 [Fic]--dc23
                    2015016331

This book is dedicated to my mom, who always found space for one more ornament.

CHAPTER 1

TWO MILES OUTSIDE THE TOWN OF RIVERTON, JESSE ALVAREZ watched his dad wrestle their Ford pickup into a sharp left turn. Just ahead, the wrought-iron gates of Savage Ranch boasted "The Finest Horses in Wyoming."

No rust on those gates. No squeaky hinges, either, he'd bet. Maybe Dad really had picked a winner this time.

The gates glided open so quickly, so smoothly, and so silently his dad didn't even need to slow down. Twisting to see out the truck's rear window, Jesse spied someone standing beside one of the tall cottonwood trees that shadowed the gates.

The man's black hair was just long enough to brush the tops of his shoulders; a red-beaded headband stretched across his forehead. His dark eyes, even at a distance, bored into Jesse's, slashing through the dust and gravel kicked up by the tires.

"Dad, I think we were supposed to stop at the gates," Jesse said. The man was waving: *Come back. Come back.* "There's a guy back there."

Mark Alvarez shot a glance at his rearview mirror.

"What guy?"

Jesse pointed through the back window.

"That…"

The driveway was empty. The man was gone.

"Long trip got you seeing things?" Mark laughed.

Jesse exhaled loudly.

"He was there, Dad. I know what I saw."

He had been bored during the eight-hour drive from Missoula, Montana to Riverton, but boredom now was giving way to annoyance. And not just with his dad for laughing at him.

He used the collar of his shirt to wipe a layer of sweat and dirt from his face. Just like the truck's power steering, the air conditioner had quit on them a couple of hundred miles back. So it was either roll up the windows and swelter or keep them down and eat dust.

Jesse poked his head out the window as they continued past clean white fences and rolling green pastures where horses grazed under wide blue skies. Grays, bays, sorrels, duns, chestnuts, paints, and palominos raised their heads as the pickup's loose fenders rattled with every bump in the road. After the truck passed, they dropped their muzzles to the grass and got back to the business of being horses.

Mark parked in front of the largest of three barns. The truck door hinges screeched as he stepped out and stretched, trying to untangle the kinks of the long drive. He gave a low whistle and shook his head in disbelief

"When we talked on the phone, Mr. Savage said his ranch was big, but I never expected anything like this."

Jesse climbed out of the passenger's seat and shielded his eyes from the late-afternoon sun. Located a short distance from each other and connected by a paved road, each barn had its own parking area, paddocks, round pens, and schooling rings. They were the nicest he had seen at any of the ranches where his dad had worked, so clean and

2

white, with green trim, green shutters, and green doors, they shimmered in the sun. He guessed each one contained twenty stalls—ten on each side facing a center aisle.

"Are you sure we're at the right place?" he asked. "I mean, look at this." He was slim, yet strongly built. He tugged at the sleeves of his shirt, which left an embarrassing inch of his wrist showing; the cuffs of his jeans were a half-inch shy of his ankles.

"There's only one Savage Ranch in Wyoming, Jess. I've got a great feeling about this. No worries this time, okay?"

Jesse nodded, automatically brushing back the lock of brown hair that fell onto his forehead. He didn't share his father's optimism. He had been the new boy at the ranch, and at school, too many times before.

Mark Alvarez came around the truck, gravel crunching underfoot, and gave Jesse's shoulders a squeeze.

"Mr. Savage is a good man, Jesse."

"Is that his house?" Jesse pointed to the immense log home that sat on a hill overlooking the ranch. The high peaks of the Wind River Mountains dominated the skyline behind the house.

Mark nodded. "Big Bob lives there with his wife and kids. Two boys, I think."

"Big Bob?"

"I hear everyone in Riverton knows Big Bob Savage," Mark laughed. "Heck, I hear everyone in the state of Wyoming knows Big Bob. He said he'd be in the big barn. Let's go find him."

Big Bob lived up to his name. He stood 6-foot-3, and looked powerful enough to wrestle a steer to the ground. He came out of the barn in the company of a younger man and strode toward Mark and Jesse, showing a smile full of white teeth. He was fit, his face tanned and a little lined.

"Mark!" Big Bob boomed, causing the horses in a nearby round pen to swivel their ears in interest. "I see you and Jesse made it in one piece. Welcome to Savage Ranch."

"It's everything you said it would be…and more, Mr. Savage."

"Oh, call me Big Bob—everyone does. Jesse…" Big Bob offered a bear-paw-sized hand. Jesse hesitated for a second before reaching to clasp it.

"Heck of a handshake you've got there, Jesse. Strong. Direct." Big Bob let go of Jesse's hand. "I'll let you in on a little secret. I know if I want to do business with a man by the time I finish shaking his hand."

"That fast?"

"Yep," Big Bob said. "Dishonest men usually give themselves away. They get nervous. You can feel it. And they rarely look you in the eye. Now, you…" Big Bob pointed at him. "…I'd do business with you any day."

Jesse smiled.

Big Bob introduced the younger man.

"This is my son Beau."

Beau smiled and touched the brim of his hat.

"Nice to meet you both."

"The foreman's office is in one of the smaller barns," Big Bob said. "Let's take a walk down there."

Jesse studied Beau as they walked to the stable. There was something familiar about him.

"Beau's my right-hand man," Big Bob said, clasping his son around the shoulders. "He's just about running things around here now he's back from college."

"That's it!" Jesse snapped his fingers. "Beau Savage! I know you! You were on the University of Wyoming rodeo team."

"Yeah, I was." Beau smiled again.

"Two-time national champ at bull-riding and roping. School record for sitting broncs. Everyone thought you were going to turn pro."

Beau shrugged. "Dad needed me."

"Yeah, but you were—are—the best."

Beau cut a sidelong glance at Big Bob.

"There's a big difference between being on a school team and trying to make it as a pro."

"With the way you ride and rope, it'd be no problem," Jesse persisted. "You'd get a sponsor so fast—they'd be lining up to put their name on your back. You'd get your own truck and trailer, and I bet a—"

"Jesse, " his dad interrupted, using his "pay-attention-to-me" tone.

Big Bob's cell phone rang, so he excused himself and walked off a few feet to take the call. Mark shook his head briskly.

Okay, I get it, Jesse thought. *You want me to drop the rodeo talk. But what's the big deal?*

Big Bob snapped the phone shut.

"Nothing like a little business deal to end the day." He looked at Beau. "Feel like driving over to John Benton's place tomorrow morning to take a look at a few fillies?"

"Sure, no problem."

"Great." Big Bob rubbed his hands together. "Beau and I are going to show your dad around the ranch, Jesse. Talk about his job a little bit and give him the quick tour, since it's getting on to dinnertime. You're welcome to tag along if you like. Or you can stay here and introduce yourself to some of my horses. Most of them are still turned out, but a few have been brought back in for the night."

"I'll stay here," Jesse said. He'd never pass on an opportunity to be around horses.

"We'll be back in about thirty minutes," Big Bob said. "Can you keep yourself busy for that long?"

"Not a problem, Mr. Savage." Jesse said. He was eager to get inside for a look at the stock.

"Great," Big Bob said. "Mark, let's start with your office."

CHAPTER 2

*JESSE STROLLED DOWN THE CENTER AISLE OF THE BARN, NOD-*ding at the ranch hands busy mucking stalls, cleaning tack, and grooming horses in crossties.

"Hey, kid, lend me a hand over here, will ya?" a lanky cowboy called out to him.

"Sure," Jesse said. "What do you need?"

"Grab hold of Belle's halter for a minute."

"Really?"

"You're walking through the middle of a stable on Savage Ranch. I reckon you know your way round a horse."

"I do."

"Good. I gotta wrap Belle's legs, but I left the tape in the tack room. Be right back."

"She's beautiful," Jesse said, stroking the chestnut mare's neck.

"That she is," the cowboy said, jogging toward the tack room. "Sixteen hands of gorgeous."

Take your time, Jesse thought.

The mare's luminous liquid-brown eyes took him in, and she nickered softy. He reached up to touch her velvety nose and was rewarded when she blew a puff of warm air onto his fingers.

Jesse was so busy with the mare it took him almost a minute to realize someone was watching him. He looked over his shoulder and saw a boy leaning against a nearby stall. The boy was blond, with ice-blue eyes that met Jesse's without blinking. A silk wild rag was tied around his neck, and his jeans were covered in dust. He held a bridle in one hand and a Stetson hat in the other.

"Hey," Jesse said, "does your dad work here, too? My dad's the new foreman. Maybe your dad will be working with mine."

The boy didn't say a word. He placed the Stetson carefully on his head so the brim shielded his eyes. He then strode past Jesse out of the barn.

"Man, what's his problem?" he asked the mare. She snorted and shook her head. "Yeah, I don't know, either."

The cowboy returned holding a roll of red Equi-Tape.

"Wanna walk her up front? There's some open crossties up there by the foreman's office."

"My dad's office," Jesse said.

"New foreman's kid, huh? Nice to meet ya. I'm Henry. You wanna visit Belle again, you just let me know."

Jesse tugged on the mare's halter to get her going. Just being close to such a fine horse made him smile.

I'd give anything to ride her, he thought.

He stopped the mare between a set of crossties. As he clipped the ties to the halter's rings he saw Big Bob, Beau, and his dad enter the barn.

"You're back already?" He blurted out. He wasn't ready to leave Belle yet.

Big Bob chuckled.

"I see you've met Henry. And he's put you to work."

"I don't mind," Jesse said.

"You got a nice way with horses," Henry said. "Thanks for the help."

Jesse gave the mare one last scratch behind her ears.

"You must have the nicest horses in Wyoming, Mr. Savage."

"I'm not going to disagree with that, Jesse," Big Bob said. He reached into his pocket and pulled out a key. "Here you go, Mark. The foreman's office is all yours."

"Thanks, Mr. Sav—Big Bob," Mark said. "See you bright and early tomorrow morning."

"I look forward to it, Mark. And Jesse, nice meeting you. Good luck at school tomorrow."

"Thanks. Oh, Mr. Savage? This might sound like a weird question, but do you have any Indian ranch hands?"

Big Bob and Beau exchanged looks.

"Why do you ask?"

"Jesse thought he saw someone down by the gates," Mark explained.

"I did see someone," Jesse insisted. "An Indian man."

"We've had men from the local Arapaho and Shoshone nations working here at one time or another," Big Bob said. "But the only Indian ranch hand here now is Jimmy Singing Bird, and he's loading bales of hay into that pickup behind you."

Jesse turned to see an older Indian man wearing a black T-shirt, jeans, and dusty cowboy boots. His hair was close-cropped and gray.

He shook his head.

"That's not him. He was wearing a headband with red and white beads."

Big Bob and Beau looked at each other again, this time for a little longer.

"Had a horse trainer here once who wore a headband like that," Big Bob said, "but that was over a year ago. It couldn't be him."

"What'd he look like?" Beau asked.

"He was a young guy, and his hair was long. It went down below his shoulders."

9

"The Wind River Reservation is just outside our gates," Big Bob said. "I reckon we just had ourselves a visitor. Happens all the time. A lot of men come our way looking for work."

CHAPTER 3

MARK AND JESSE LEFT THE STABLE AND STARTED BACK TO their truck.

"Did you have a good time looking around?" Mark asked. "Are you as impressed as I am with Savage Ranch?"

"Yeah," Jesse said, "how could I not be? Temperature-controlled stalls, automatic waterers, mats in the center aisles…The horses here aren't like any I've been around before, either. They're sleek and glossy, like movie stars. You can't stop staring at them. Even the ranch horses are amazing. Oh, and I met some kid. Wouldn't talk to me."

"Shy, maybe?"

Jesse considered this.

"No," he decided, "something else."

"What do you think about Big Bob?"

"Well, you sure can tell he's the boss. But he's nice. I like him."

"I like him, too," Mark said. "He's not like any boss I've had before. He's the first to see me as a foreman."

"That's so cool you've got your own office. Cool about Beau being here, too. I remember hearing on the radio how he was all set to turn pro and join the Wyoming state team. Wonder why he didn't?"

"I guess that's between Big Bob and Beau," Mark said. "I kind of get the feeling that, nice as he is, what Big Bob wants, Big Bob gets."

"Yeah, I got that, too. So, where's the bunkhouse?"

A wide grin spread across his father's face.

"Ranch hands live in a bunkhouse. The foreman gets his own house."

"We have a house?" Jesse paused with the truck door halfway open and stared at his father. "No way."

"Get in."

They took a narrow dirt road past the stables. Around a small bend, through a cluster of pine and cottonwood trees, Jesse saw a small white-shingled house. It was private and peaceful; mule deer grazed along the edge of the woods, and the only noise came from the birds in the trees and a stream gurgling behind the house.

"Feeds into the Shoshone River," Mark said with a nod toward the stream.

The house couldn't compare to the one owned by the Savage family, but Jesse was still amazed he and his dad would have it to themselves. He dashed up onto the front porch.

"Door's open," he called.

Mark Alvarez bounded up and followed Jesse through the front door. The house was neat and clean and nicely, although not expensively, furnished right down to sheets on the beds, towels in the bathroom, and silverware and dishes in the kitchen. A good thing, too, since what little the Alvarez men owned fit in their truck.

The house had a living room with a stone fireplace, a kitchen big enough to eat in, one large bathroom, and two bedrooms. Large area rugs with a Western design covered the hardwood floors. And the place was immaculate. The kitchen counter and sink gleamed, and there wasn't a speck of dust on the couch, floor, or any of the end tables.

Jesse wandered over to the fridge and swung the door open. It was packed with food.

"Wow. Where'd all this come from?" He pulled out a glass pitcher for a closer look. "Someone even made iced tea for us. Think it was Mrs. Savage?"

"I do," Mark said. "She must be a thoughtful woman."

The cabinets and the bread drawer were also full.

"You know, I'm suddenly hungry," Jesse said.

"Me, too," Mark said. He rifled through the boxes, bottles, and cans in the cabinets. "Let's do something easy, like spaghetti. I'm bushed from the drive."

They worked together, boiling water for the pasta and setting the table.

"That smells good." Mark leaned in to smell the sauce Jesse was stirring on the stove.

"It's from a jar." Jesse spoke quietly. "Not like Mom's homemade sauce." He tapped the spoon against the rim of the pot and laid it on the counter. "I dream about Mom sometimes. She's in the kitchen making her spaghetti sauce, and she calls me to come and taste it. I run and run, but the hallway just gets longer. I always wake up without finding her."

"I know you miss her."

"She'd like this house, don't you think?" Jesse asked. "I bet she'd come visit us if she knew we had a house."

"Next time she calls, you can tell her all about it."

Jesse nodded and went to the cabinet to grab some glasses. He didn't mention his mom again. He'd learned a long time ago that pestering his dad wouldn't get him everything he wanted.

After dinner, Mark rubbed his full belly and stood up.

"Better unpack," he said. "You take the big bedroom, Jess. I'm going to get you a desk for your schoolwork. We'll pick up some new jeans and school clothes, too. You're already growing out of everything I just bought."

"Okay, Dad."

He went into his new bedroom and flopped backwards onto the bed. He could hear the stream through the closed window. It was a comforting sound, and it made him feel sleepy...

Blinking hard, Jesse sat up; daylight was fading, but it was still too early to go to bed. He stared at the bare walls and thought about his rolled-up rodeo posters out in the truck. Experience had taught him he wouldn't stick around long enough to bother putting any personal touches on his bedroom. He wanted to believe—and he already felt—that this time would be different.

For now, though, the walls would remain bare, and the posters would remain rolled up in the back of the truck.

He wandered over to the window, pulled up the shade...

And stared into the same dark eyes he had seen earlier when they'd passed through the gates of Savage Ranch. The young Indian man stood a short distance away on the stream bank. In the second or so it took for Jesse to think about calling his dad, the man vanished. Again.

CHAPTER 4

JESSE JUMPED OFF THE BUS IN FRONT OF HIS NEW MIDDLE school early the next morning with the same old questions running through his mind: Where will I sit? Will anyone talk to me? Will I fit in? This was not the first time he had changed schools after the year had begun. No matter how many times he did it, it didn't get any easier.

After a quick stop in the office to get his class schedule, he joined the crowd of kids jostling for space in the hallway. Teenage voices, locker doors clanging shut, and PA announcements bombarded his ears. Most kids ignored him, but some stared. He found his first-period classroom, took a deep breath, and walked in.

He grabbed the first empty seat he saw and pulled his notebook out of his backpack. So far, so good. He sat back and relaxed a little.

A girl walked over and stood right in front of him. The headband holding back her long white-blond hair matched the deep blue of her eyes. She smiled with perfect white teeth.

Jesse smiled back.

"You're new," she said.

He could only nod. Sometimes his brain and his mouth wouldn't work at the same time when he was near a girl he thought was pretty.

"What's your name?"

"Um…Jesse…Yeah, Jesse." For a moment, he wasn't sure. But, hey, if this girl wanted to talk to him, maybe another new school wouldn't be so bad.

"You're in my seat, Jesse," the girl said.

"Oh, right…right…sorry." He leapt up, his face flushing at the sound of laughter ringing in his ears.

"Oh, snap!" a girl seated behind Jesse said. "Lexi, you are so mean! Hassling the new kid."

"Like you don't throw a fit if someone even looks at *your* seat." Lexi rolled her eyes. She slid into the chair and started to unpack her books without another glance at Jesse.

He stood awkwardly by the door as the rest of the class filed in and took their seats. He pretended to be interested in his schedule, but how long could you stare at the same piece of paper without looking stupid?

The teacher, Miss Miller, came into the classroom as the first-period bell rang. Stragglers were now flying down the hallway, hoping to get to class before the doors closed and they were marked tardy. Miss Miller smiled at Jesse and motioned for him to stand with her at the front of the room.

"Class," she said, loudly enough to get her students' attention, "we have a new student joining us." She placed a hand on Jesse's shoulder. "This is Jesse Alvarez."

Jesse stole a glance at Lexi; she was turning the pages of her binder, not even paying attention.

"Why don't you tell us a little something about yourself, Jesse," Miss Miller continued. "Help us get to know you."

"Well…um…we just moved here from Montana," Jesse stammered. He didn't like being on display.

"What brings your family to Wyoming?" Miss Miller asked.

"My dad got a new job."

"Well, I look forward to meeting your parents."

"No, ma'am. I mean, it's just me and my dad. Just my dad." Jesse frowned. Did he really have to stand up here and talk about such private family matters?

"Thank you for sharing that with us, Jesse," Miss Miller said. "Let's find you a seat and begin class."

"Miss Miller! Miss Miller!" The voice came from the second row next to the windows. A small boy with shiny jet-black hair waved his hand frantically in the air. "Jesse can sit in back of me. There's an empty desk behind mine. See? No one's sat there since Ryan moved to Cheyenne."

"No one *wants* to sit there," a boy in the back of the room called out. A few kids snickered.

"That's a great idea, Aaron," Miss Miller said.

"Aw, Aaron's got a friend now, " the same boy said. Loud laughter broke out across the class.

"That's enough, Luke," Miss Miller said sharply.

Jesse slid into his new seat, opened his notebook, and pulled out his pencil. Aaron turned around and grinned at him.

"Hi!" he said. "I'm Aaron Little Elk. Aren't these great seats, right by the window? I love sitting by the window. There's always something to see..."

The boy yammered on as if he weren't in a classroom and didn't have a teacher standing in front of him. Jesse heard whispers and muffled laughter start up again.

He interrupted Aaron's monologue.

"Yeah, maybe you should turn around now."

He wanted less attention from his new classmates, not more.

The corners of Aaron's mouth turned down. He slumped in his seat.

Jesse leaned over his desk. He'd regretted his words as soon as he had said them. He didn't want to hurt Aaron. He knew what it was like to be taunted in school, and he hoped he hadn't made Aaron feel the same way.

"I just don't want you to get in trouble for talking because of me," he whispered. He had noticed the desk in front of Aaron was empty, too. Didn't this kid have *any* friends?

"It's all right." Aaron waved Jesse's apology away with one hand. "Reuben says I talk so much I even talk in my sleep!"

"Who's Reu—"

"Boys and girls," Miss Miller called over the whispering voices around the room, "please do your warm-up quietly while I take roll."

Aaron turned around to face the front. Notebooks and binders were opened, and the sound of pencils scratching on paper replaced the whispers. Jesse sighed in relief and looked at the board at the front of the room. The warm-up was a math problem. Okay, he could handle this. Math and science were his favorite subjects. He knew they would be important if he wanted to become a veterinarian.

He tuned out the sound of Miss Miller taking roll while he concentrated on the math problem. There would be time later to learn names. Only when he finished did he sit back and listen to the end of the roll call.

"Jamison Robey."

"Here."

"Carla Sanderson."

"Here."

"Cade Savage."

Jesse sat straight up in his seat. Savage? He scanned the room until he found himself looking into the same ice-blue eyes he had seen yesterday in the barn at Savage Ranch.

"Here," Cade Savage said, returning Jesse's gaze.

18

So, the unfriendly boy was not the son of a ranch hand, but the son of the boss. Jesse smiled and nodded. Cade Savage curled his lip and turned away.

I still don't get it, Jesse thought. *What is his problem?*

CHAPTER 5

GRIPPING HIS BROWN-BAG LUNCH AND THE PINT OF CHOCO-
late milk he had just purchased, Jesse carefully scanned the
cafeteria for an available seat. No way did he want to give
an encore of this morning's embarrassing performance of
grabbing the first empty seat he saw.

Cade Savage's table was out, and not just because it was
already packed with boys. Jesse recognized them—the popu-
lar kids. It wasn't something he had to be told; it was something any kid in any school would know.

Cade and his friends sat like they owned the air around
them. Their boisterous laughter could be heard across the
entire cafeteria. They talked loudly, not caring who heard
them. They took "basketball shots" at the trashcans with
their crumpled-up bags and empty milk and juice cartons,
not even bothering to get up and retrieve the trash when
they missed. They were totally locked onto each other. No
one else in the cafeteria mattered.

Already ten minutes late to lunch because he'd forgot-
ten the last number of his new locker combination then
couldn't find the cafeteria, Jesse wanted a seat fast.

He noticed a table against the wall that had a few empty seats; one of the boys sitting there caught his eye and nodded. Jesse had started over when, out of the corner of his eye, he saw an arm frantically waving at him.

It was Aaron Little Elk.

"Over here! New boy…Jesse! I saved you a seat!"

A seat? There wasn't one other kid sitting at that table. Jesse continued toward the table by the wall, thinking Aaron would give up and quiet down.

He didn't. He yelled Jesse's name louder and waved both of his arms in the air. By now, every kid in the lunchroom was staring at Jesse. He could hear the laughter coming from Cade Savage's table.

He turned on his heel and strode toward Aaron. He dropped his math book on the table, smiling in satisfaction when it landed with a bang that made Aaron flinch. He slid in across from Aaron and began, wordlessly, to eat his lunch.

"Jeez, what's with you?" Aaron asked. He wiped chocolate milk off his mouth with the back of his hand.

When Jesse didn't answer, Aaron shrugged and stuffed a chicken nugget in his mouth. He then wiped his hands on his pants.

"Want some ice cream from the snack line," he asked Jesse, "or some chips?"

"I don't have any money."

"Don't need any. I've got a number I punch into a little machine at the cash register. It works like magic. We can get anything we want. I never have to pay."

Jesse knew all about the "magic" numbers. He'd had a number at his old school, a few years back in fifth grade. It had allowed him to get free breakfast and lunch in the school cafeteria. Mark Alvarez had lost his job when a horse kicked him and fractured his left leg in three places. The ranch owner had taken Jesse in while his father was in the hospital, but he couldn't pay a man who couldn't work.

22

Social workers had talked to Mark, bringing mounds of paperwork and offers of "assistance" and "programs." Then the number had come in the mail. His father told him not to be embarrassed. Things would be a little rough until he could find work again, but tough times didn't last forever.

Jesse had hated using the number.; he'd tried walking slowly to the cafeteria so he could be last in line and no one but the cashier would see him punch it in. But he couldn't manage that every day; he usually wound up standing in the middle of the lunch line, surrounded by kids who held cash in their hands.

Aaron stood up.

"Last chance. I'm getting another ice cream."

"No, thanks, I don't want anything. And the snack lines are closing. Bell's going to ring in about ten minutes."

"Darn," Aaron said, "now I have to wait until tomorrow to get some chips and ice cream.

"It's not the end of the world, Aaron. Just get some snacks at home."

"The magic number only works at school, Jesse. It can't make snacks appear at home." Aaron gathered his trash and left to dump it, leaving Jesse sitting at the table staring after him.

CHAPTER 6

PE WAS THE LAST CLASS OF THE DAY.

"Soccer today, guys and gals, we're going outside," Mr. Felton said. "Alvarez, you're the new kid, right? Grab a uniform out of my office. Take locker number one-thirty-two."

It took Jesse a few minutes to find both shorts and a T-shirt in his size. He ran into the locker room, where most of the boys were already on their way outside. He changed quickly, shoved his clothes and books into his locker, and sprinted out the gym door into the bright afternoon sunlight.

Mr. Felton stood in front of the class with his clipboard.

"Let's see." He flipped a few pages. "Luke Wilson, you're a captain. Becky Davis, you're a captain. If you pick a boy first, your next pick is a girl. You pick a girl first; your next pick is a boy. Got it? Go."

Luke won the coin toss.

"Cade," he called.

"Big surprise," Aaron muttered.

It was Becky's turn next.

"Jen," she said.

Jen pumped her fist.

"Yeah!"

Becky and Jen looked strong and athletic. The idea of the competition being close spiked Jesse's interest.

"Hey, this might be fun," he said to Aaron.

"If you say so." Aaron stood with both arms crossed over his chest.

Luke scanned the group of hopefuls standing before him.

"Lexi," he called.

"Another surprise…not," Aaron said.

Jen whispered into Becky's ear. Becky, nodding and grinning, made her next pick.

"Jesse," she said.

Every head swiveled toward Jesse. A low *ooh* sounded.

"Cut it out," Mr. Felton said.

Becky and Luke picked quickly until there were only two kids left—Aaron and a tiny, pale girl named Ivy who sneezed constantly.

"Mr. Felton," she whined, "my allergies."

"Don't even think about asking, Ivy," Mr. Felton said, scribbling on his clipboard. "You've been to see the nurse too many times. You've got to start participating if you want a grade."

Luke said, "We don't need any more players. Becky can have Aaron and Ivy."

"Nice try," said Mr. Felton. "Aaron, you're on Luke's team. Ivy, you go to Becky's."

Both teams moaned, but they didn't challenge him.

"Aaron," Cade called as he trotted out to the midfield line to join Luke and take the ball at kickoff, "you're slow, and you can't kick. Everyone knows it, so, don't argue. Get in the goal."

"That's a bad idea," Lexi said, "even with extra defenders. I'll play goalie."

"You're too fast to waste in the goal," Cade countered. "We need you up front."

Jen and Becky watched from the sideline. After a brief whispered conversation, Jen called a team huddle.

"Here's the plan—attack, attack, attack the goal all day long."

"What about Aaron?" Jesse asked.

"What about him?" Jen gave him a cool look. "He's on the other team," she said, as if explaining something to a young child.

"Yeah, yeah, I get that," Jesse said. "I mean, why would Cade put Aaron in the goal?"

"Because," Jen said, "Cade Savage is a butthead who doesn't think we'll get past his awesome defense to even get a shot on Aaron. We're going to show him just how wrong he is. I know you and Aaron are friends—"

"I just met Aaron today," Jesse interrupted, "so it's not like we're really friends."

"That's great," Jen said dismissively. "Becks, you play out on the right, Jesse, you play out on the left. I'll play center forward, and I'll serve the ball to you two. Easy goals. Just watch the offsides."

"Uh, what about us?" Ben Cottrell asked.

"Anyone else gets the ball, play it over to me or back to me," Jen said. "Ivy, just wander around, or something."

"But what do I do?" Ivy asked.

"Pick flowers, make origami butterflies out of your tissues, I don't care. Just stay away from the ball."

"Like I want to play this stupid game anyway," Ivy said. "I can't believe we get graded for this." She split off from the group and sneezed her way out to the field.

The game was intense and close. Toward the end of class, the score was 1-0 in favor of Cade's team. Cade had scored his team's single goal, and so far, the team's defense *had* protected Aaron. Jesse had had a few good opportunities, but the sight of Aaron all alone in the goal made him hold back, and his shots, although strong and on target, sailed over the goal.

Jen noticed.

"Jesse," she said. "You're getting through their defense, and you've got a great shot, but you're playing it way too safe. Their defense is tiring out from protecting Aaron. They're so worried you're getting shots on Aaron they're leaving me completely alone and unmarked. Let's use that. We need a goal."

"I know," Jesse said. He wanted to win, but he didn't want to give Cade and his buddies another reason to torture Aaron.

"Look," Jen said, "let me put it this way. Do you want to lose to Cade Savage and that parade of morons he calls friends? 'Cause I know I don't."

That was all it took.

"Pass me the ball," Jesse said. "Try and put it a little ahead of me on the left so I can pick it up with my left foot."

"Will do." Jen clapped him on the back. "Hey, have some fun and mess with Cade a little bit. Run past him and get him turned facing his own goal. Then come back onsides. Like I said, they're not even marking me. I'll have plenty of time to pass you the ball."

Jesse laughed. He was beginning to like Jen, although he still found himself stealing glances at Lexi.

Jen's pass was right on the money; Jesse made sure he was back onside before she let it fly off the end of her foot. He gathered the ball and dribbled straight at Cade, who was now so off-balance he had no hope of catching Jesse. It was an out-and-out sprint for the goal before the game ended.

Out of the corner of his eye, Jesse saw Luke streaking in to challenge him; he never broke his stride. He stutter-stepped with the ball, getting Luke to pull up and try to guess which direction he was going to take. Jesse faked to the left, went right, and dodged around Luke.

There was nobody now between Jesse and Aaron in the goal.

"Hands up!" he heard Cade shrieking. "Block the shot, Aaron!"

About thirty feet out, Jesse shifted his weight to his right leg. He threw his arms out to the side for balance then drew his left leg back and fired a shot. This time, he aimed it directly at the goal. The ball went in hard and fast.

Aaron's eyes widened. He ducked, covering his head with his hands. The ball sailed into the back of the net, giving Jesse's team the tying goal.

CHAPTER 7

THE TEAM ERUPTED INTO CHEERS AND SCREAMS OF PURE JOY.
Jen and Becky high-fived each other.

Jen jogged over to Jesse and punched him—not lightly—on the arm.

"Way to go, Jesse. 'Bout time we got some decent soccer players around here," she said loudly enough for Cade to hear. She danced around Cade and Luke, her brunette ponytail bouncing and her arms outstretched, palms up, as if to say, "What now, boys?"

"Well done, Jesse," Mr. Felton said. "That was a nice shot. Aaron, way to stand tall in the goal. I don't think I could've stopped that one. Nice try."

"Nice try?" Cade exploded. "What 'try?' Rez-boy didn't even put his hands up. He ducked!"

"Enough!" There was no mistaking the anger in the teacher's voice. "You've just crossed a line, Mr. Savage. You will not talk to or about anyone in this school like that. Do you understand me?"

Cade glared at Mr. Felton, kicking angrily at the ground.

"Answer me, Cade, or I *will* call your parents. I know them, and they will not be pleased."

"Yes," Cade finally said.

"Good. Class is over," Mr. Felton said. "Game's a tie."

"But you had the whistle in your mouth before Jesse even took that shot. I saw you," Cade argued. "The game should have ended then!"

Luke walked up to his friend.

"Cade, man, let it go. You had a great goal. We'll get these wimps next time."

Cade shrugged him off and turned his attention back to Aaron.

"Why did you duck like that? You should have stood your ground."

"And let someone kick a ball in my face?" Aaron shot back.

"You're supposed to stop it! You're the goalie."

"That wasn't my idea," Aaron said. "Seems kind of stupid to let someone kick a ball at your face."

"Yeah, well, it's only stupid 'cause you suck at it."

"Well, Reuben says…"

"Shut up about Reuben," Cade said. "What's wrong with you?"

"Boys," Mr. Felton called, "Savage, Little Elk, let's go! Time's wasting; the bell for dismissal is about to ring."

Cade trotted off in the direction of the boys' locker room. He glanced back at Aaron over his shoulder.

"Loser," he spat.

Jesse changed out of his PE uniform and back into his clothes. He crammed the uniform into the small locker, grabbed his books, and headed out of the gym. At the dismissal bell, he joined the crowds spilling out of the front door of the school.

Sighting Lexi, he slowed his pace as he approached her.

Think of something good to say, he thought. *Got to make up for taking her seat this morning.*

32

A raucous burst of laughter stopped him in his tracks. A group of boys standing behind a large oak tree had some kid surrounded. Veering away from Lexi, he tried to get closer to the tree so he could hear what was going on.

"Leave me alone! I'll tell Reuben."

"You do that. Let us know what he says."

"Hey, why don't you tell Reuben to get you a haircut? You look like a girl, bangs all in your eyes."

"Nah, I think Aaron looks more like a sheepdog."

"Mangy sheepdog, you mean. Only kind they got out on the Rez."

Jesse recognized those voices. Walking around the tree, he saw Aaron in the middle of the group. Larger kids surrounded him—Cade Savage, Luke Wilson, and, as Jen had put it, their parade of moron friends.

This is none of my business, Jesse thought. *It's my first day here, and Cade Savage, for some reason, already doesn't like me. I really don't want to make an enemy of the boss's son.*

Besides, Cade and Luke wouldn't actually hurt Aaron. They were probably just giving him a hard time about the soccer game.

Head down, he started to walk by the group. He didn't get more than ten feet before a sense of shame began to creep over him. He knew the boys were bullying Aaron. He would never stand by and let a horse be threatened or abused, so, why would he let Aaron be?

I'm going to regret this, Jesse told himself. *I just know I am.*

He took a deep breath and turned to face Cade and his friends.

"Hey, what's going on, Aaron?"

"Aw," Luke taunted, "rescuing your lunch buddy. How sweet."

"No," Jesse said. "I just wondered if we were all walking to the bus stop together."

"Yeah," Luke said, "we're going the same way, but…" He elbowed Cade. "…I don't think Cade walks with the hired help."

Cade picked his backpack up by one strap and slung it over his shoulder.

"I don't ride the bus, Alvarez, my mom picks me up. But, sure, you can walk with me—as long as you stay about twenty feet behind. I'll drop some candy wrappers and tissues on the ground so you can practice doing your dad's job."

Jesse's face flushed with anger. He took a deep breath.

"My father," he said slowly, "is the foreman."

"Foreman, trash man, what's the difference?" Cade smirked. "Just another employee on my dad's ranch." He roughly brushed between Aaron and Jesse and sauntered off without looking back.

"Hey, wait up!" Luke called. He grabbed his backpack and took off after Cade. "Bye, girls," he said to Aaron and Jesse. "Hold hands on the way home."

CHAPTER 8

JESSE BOARDED THE SCHOOL BUS WITH AARON RIGHT BEHIND him. He went to the back and slid into a seat next to a window. Aaron slid in after him.

Jesse watched Cade and Luke join another group of kids; Lexi was among them. Cade and Lexi split off and walked toward Ellie Savage's huge white SUV. Luke followed at a short distance, kicking up dust as he walked.

"Do they mess with you every day?" Jesse asked.

"Just about," Aaron said as the bus lurched forward then rumbled out onto the highway. "But not always."

"What jerks!"

"Nah, they're not always like that."

Jesse couldn't believe his ears.

"You're kidding," he said. "You do know they were making fun of you."

"Duh, Jesse, I'm not stupid. But Reuben says they're not that important. Reuben says to ignore them and not let them get to me. So, I do. He says Cade Savage is a miserable person who wants to make other people as miserable as him."

"Who's Reuben?"

"My big brother. When something bothers me, I just tell Reuben. I can tell him anything, and he always knows what to do. He's smart. He finished high school."

"Most people finish high school."

"Maybe in your family."

Aaron turned away, staring at the Wind River Mountains through the window across the aisle. Jesse began to worry he'd offended him, but then the boy's face brightened.

"I didn't even tell you the best part. Reuben is just about the best horse trainer in the world. Even Big Bob thinks so. He was one of Big Bob's best trainers."

"He worked for Big Bob?" Jesse asked. "Wow. He sounds cool."

"Oh, he is, Jesse. He's the best brother in the world. You'll see when you meet him. Sometimes he drives me home from school so I don't have to take the bus."

"Do kids on the bus bother you, too?"

Aaron shrugged. "Depends on who the driver is."

"I bet Cade and Luke don't bother you when Reuben's here," Jesse said. "I met Cade's big brother, Beau. He doesn't seem anything like Cade."

"Nope, he's nice," Aaron agreed. "Cade's probably so mean 'cause his brother is good at everything and he's not. Big Bob's always bragging about Beau." He slumped back against the seat and looked up at Jesse. "We're friends, aren't we? Now that we know each other, I mean."

"We don't know each other. We just met."

"Is it 'cause I'm a Shoshone?"

"What? No. I know lots of Indians."

"Well, some people are funny about it. In every grade, whenever we're learning about American history, the teacher will say, 'Oh, Aaron, why don't you do a report on Sacajawea. She was a Shoshone *just like you!*'"

Jesse could see Savage Ranch through the trees in the distance.

"Guess I'll see you tomorrow," he said. "This is my stop."

"Mine, too," Aaron said, hopping into the aisle while the bus was still moving. He swayed and almost toppled over as the bus slowed and then squeaked to a stop.

"Young man," the bus driver called, his eyes on the rearview mirror, "next time stay in your seat until the bus comes to a complete stop."

A whoosh sounded as the driver opened the doors. Jesse took the steps two at a time, jumping out on the dusty road. Aaron followed right behind him.

"Doesn't the bus go all the way to the reservation?" Jesse asked. "You must have a long way to walk."

"It's not that bad, and anyway, I know a shortcut." Aaron regarded Jesse with a thoughtful look. "Reuben says you can tell a lot about horses just by observing what they do naturally. Same for people. You could have scored a ton of goals on me today, but you didn't."

"One was enough," Jesse said. "I've only lived here two days, and I already hate the idea of losing to Cade Savage." Feeling the weight of his new textbooks, Jesse let his backpack slip off his shoulder for a moment. For the first time, he noticed that Aaron carried no backpack.

"Didn't you bring any books home?"

"Nope."

"Aren't you going to do your homework?"

Aaron didn't answer.

"What does Reuben say about that?" Jesse asked. "He wouldn't have graduated from high school without doing his home—"

"I've got something for you," Aaron interrupted. He jammed a hand into his pants pocket and pulled out a wad of yarn, string, and feathers wound around a small hoop. As he began to slowly and carefully straighten its strands, the object took a familiar shape.

"It's a dreamcatcher," Jesse said.

Aaron nodded. "Yep. Made it myself. I want you to have it."

"It's too nice to just give away," Jesse said. "I mean, we just met and all…"

Aaron thrust the dreamcatcher into Jesse's hands.

"Take it," he said. "Hang it over your bed. They trap bad dreams…sad dreams."

Jesse blinked. Surely, Aaron wasn't talking about…

"Gotta go." Aaron said suddenly. And then he *was* gone. At the same time he disappeared into the slender rays of sunlight streaming through the canopy of cottonwood and pine trees, the dark-haired man Jesse had seen outside of his bedroom window stepped out.

Jeez, Jesse wondered, *how long is this guy just going to hang around before he asks Big Bob for a job?*

CHAPTER 9

JESSE DUG HIS KEY OUT OF THE BOTTOM OF HIS BACKPACK and let himself into the house.

"Dad? Dad?" *Not here, must still be working.*

He threw his backpack onto the kitchen table, grabbed a Coke from the fridge, and flopped down on the couch. In a few minutes, he'd tackle his homework before starting dinner, but he wanted some time to think back over the day. He was reliving his soccer goal when someone knocked on the door.

He swung the door open to find a tall, slim woman holding a foil-covered glass dish. She wore fine, hand-tooled boots and denims with stiff creases. Turquoise-and-silver bracelets ringed her wrists. Her auburn hair, under a Stetson, gleamed in the afternoon sun.

"Hello," she said, stepping into the living room. "I wanted to pop by and see how the newest recruits to Savage Ranch were getting on."

"Just fine, ma'am."

"Glad to hear it." She held out the casserole dish. "I brought you and your dad a little something. I just made some for my family—it's their favorite. I hope you like it, too."

Jesse took the dish. Whatever was inside smelled wonderful, and his stomach growled in anticipation.

"Thank you, ma'am. That's really kind of you."

"I'll get the dish later, no rush." She turned toward the front door. "Guess I'll be going. Got a new gelding to see to—he's coming along nicely."

"Do you work for Mr. Savage?"

"You could certainly say that." She laughed. "I'm Ellie Savage, Jesse. Mr. Savage is my husband."

Jesse winced with embarrassment, but she pretended not to notice.

"I understand you're quite the horseman yourself, Jesse."

"I've been around them my whole life. What are you training the gelding for?"

"He's my newest barrel-racing prospect."

Jesse flinched. His mind jumped to the framed picture on the desk in his bedroom, and for a few seconds he couldn't speak. The picture showed his mom sitting on a horse, a blue ribbon in her hand.

"Oh," he finally whispered.

"You're not a fan?"

"It's just that… It's…." He swiped at his eyes. "My mom was a barrel racer. I used to watch her when I was little."

"She stopped?"

"A long time ago."

"I bet she was great."

"She was."

Jesse decided he liked Ellie Savage. She looked at him when he talked, and she listened—something that, in his experience, adults didn't always do.

She was halfway out the door when she suddenly turned.

"We're holding a race here next month. Come watch."

He smiled. "I will."

"I'll be expecting you, then. Cade will be there."

"Who?"

"Cade. My son."

Oh, yeah— Cade.

"We're in the same class at school," he said.

Ellie Savage frowned.

"Oh? Cade didn't mention that when I picked him up today."

"Probably just slipped his mind."

"Well, I hope Cade remembered his manners and helped you on your first day, Jesse. He can certainly show you how things work around school."

"Oh, he did. I understand exactly how things work around school."

CHAPTER 10

JESSE STUFFED A TURKEY SANDWICH, THREE COOKIES, AND AN apple into the brown paper bag. He quickly surveyed the kitchen; the breakfast dishes were washed and stacked, and the counters were wiped. His father, as was usual for ranch work, had left before sunrise.

Despite the many years this had been the Alvarez men's morning routine, Jesse was still not used to the stillness of the house, the absolute quiet as he ate breakfast alone almost every day. He had asked—no, begged—for a dog, but his father pointed out that it wouldn't be fair to get an animal and then leave it alone most of the day.

He looped his backpack over one shoulder, grabbed his lunch, and headed for the door.

The first few weeks at Savage Ranch had flown by. He'd even taken the rodeo posters out of the car and covered his walls. He had also accepted that, even if he didn't understand the reason, he and Cade Savage were probably never going to be friends.

Sighing, Jesse opened the front door. Aaron Little Elk was sitting on the front porch.

"I was beginning to think you'd never come out," he said.

"If I'd known you were out here, I might not have." He wasn't serious. Well, maybe half-serious.

Since his first day at school, everyone, including the teachers, had assumed he and Aaron were best friends. He liked Aaron, but lately the boy had been showing up at the house very early in the morning, even on days when there was no school. Usually, Jesse would find him just as he had today—curled up on the porch watching the front door. On other days, the only clue Aaron had been there was the homemade dreamcatcher he left on the top step of the porch. Jesse placed each one in the top drawer of his dresser.

He strode past Aaron toward the path that led to the bus stop.

"What are you doing here, anyway?" he asked, his voice a bit harsher than he'd intended.

"Waiting for you, duh. Hey, hold up!"

Aaron broke into a run to catch up. Jesse stopped and turned to face him.

"How did you get here?"

"Walked, duh. Same as yesterday. And the day before."

"Stop saying 'duh,' okay? It's really annoying."

Jesse started walking again. Was this what having a little brother was like? Maybe silence in the morning wasn't such a bad thing after all.

"You don't live around here. Not even close. And the school bus goes to the reservation. So, why do you keep walking all the way to my house?"

"'Cause we're best friends, d—" Aaron clasped a hand over his mouth. "That was close. I almost said 'duh' again."

"You *are* my friend, Aaron. But so are Mike, and Logan. I don't really have a best friend. I just have…friends."

"Are you serious? I mean, do you have amnesia or something?" Aaron's voice took on a patient tone. "You sit at the

44

desk behind me in math class. We sit at the same table in art class and during lunch. We walk to the bus stop together."

"That's the thing," Jesse said. "I want to start sitting at Mike and Logan's lunch table. I'm sure they wouldn't mind if you sit there, too."

"They don't want me at their table, Jesse. You know they don't. They asked you, not me."

"I'll talk to them."

"No, don't."

"Aaron…"

"It's okay, Jesse, we're still friends. I'm not mad. Do you still want to go fishing with me and Reuben? 'Cause he said he'd take us to Boysen Reservoir."

"Yeah, of course, I do. I already asked my dad. Just tell me when."

"Soon," Aaron said. "Reuben said soon."

He didn't say much as they continued on to the bus stop, but he didn't seem upset. He walked with Jesse in the hallways and worked with him on a social studies project.

At lunch, Jesse sat with Logan and Mike.

"Jesse, can you come over my house this weekend?" Mike asked. "Logan's coming. My dad's gonna take us out on the ATVs."

"I'll have to ask my dad, but I'm sure he'll say yes," Jesse said, excited at the thought of riding an ATV.

He had met both Mike and Logan at school, but he saw a lot of them at Savage Ranch as well. Logan's dad was a farrier and Mike's dad was an equine veterinarian; both boys often accompanied their dads on regular visits to the ranch to care for Big Bob's horses. Jesse was impressed that Logan actually helped his dad shoe the horses and care for their feet and hooves.

But he especially loved to tag along with Mike and his dad; when he felt he wasn't in the way, Jesse peppered the veterinarian with questions about his job.

Working visits to Savage Ranch sometimes took hours to complete because Big Bob owned so many horses. Even after the work was done, Big Bob would spend time just standing around jawing with the two men. That had given Jesse plenty of time to discover how much he had in common with Logan and Mike.

All three boys liked soccer, fishing, and camping—just about any outdoor activity; but they especially bonded over their love of horses. They roamed Big Bob's pastures and paddocks talking about the horses they owned, the ones they hoped to someday own, and their plans for the future. Logan wanted to complete high school and join his dad as a farrier. Jesse wanted to be a large animal veterinarian specializing in equine medicine. He assumed Mike wanted to be a veterinarian like his dad.

"A vet? No way," Mike had said. "I'm going to the University of Wyoming. Gonna be a star on the rodeo team. Just like Beau Savage. Only difference is I'm going to turn pro. I'll get sponsored and make tons of money."

"The Junior Rodeo's coming up soon, Jesse," Logan had added. "We both ride. You should check it out, too."

CHAPTER 11

As the lunch period ended, Jesse got up to throw his trash away and saw Aaron sitting alone at a table in the back of the cafeteria. He was staring at something on his lunch tray, which was littered with potato chip bags and ice cream wrappers. Aaron looked up and met Jesse's gaze. A wide smile broke out across the boy's face, and he waved enthusiastically at Jesse as if he were across a field and not just a school cafeteria.

Why is he smiling? Jesse wondered. *Why can't he be mad at me? Why doesn't he call me a jerk for abandoning him? Then maybe I wouldn't feel so bad.*

He was about to walk over to say hi to Aaron when Mike and Logan jumped in front of him.

"Jesse, c'mon, you gotta see this." Mike grabbed his sleeve. "It just went up a few minutes ago."

"It's what we've been telling you about," Logan added.

They walked a short distance down the hall to the library, where a group of students crowded around a poster on the wall. Jesse edged in closer to get a look.

JUNIOR RODEO

Saturday, June 1st
Savage Fairgrounds

Calf Roping
¼-mile Race
Broncs
Barrel Racing

$300 First Place cash prize for each event!

ENTER TODAY

"Savage Fairgrounds?" Jesse said. "Is there anything that doesn't have their name on it?"

"Not around here." Mike laughed.

Cade Savage muscled through the crowd until he was right in front of the poster.

"You ride, Alvarez?" Cade asked.

"Yeah, do you?"

The other boys exploded in laughter. One playfully punched Jesse on the arm.

"Dude, you really are new around here!"

"No one beats Cade at rodeo," Luke said. "No one."

"That true?" Jesse asked.

"Damn right," Cade said.

"Then how come the only Savage I hear about when it comes to rodeo is Beau?"

Cade's face reddened

"I'm pretty good," Jesse continued.

"You need a horse to rope and race, Alvarez. You know that, right?" Cade said. "And I didn't see a horse crammed in the back of your dad's crap wagon when you moved in."

"I don't have my own horse," Jesse admitted.

"Too bad," Cade said. "Sucks being poor, huh? Guess you'll never be able to prove how good you are."

"Your dad could loan him one, Cade," one of the boys piped up. "Your family has so many horses."

"I don't need anybody's charity," Jesse said, staring directly at Cade.

"My dad already gave to charity when he hired yours." Cade smirked. "But that's the way my dad is, always ready to help some outta-work, homeless stable boy who's down on his luck."

Luke patted Cade's shoulder.

"Dude, your dad's a saint."

"Practically," Cade agreed. "Especially when you can't even be sure this particular stable boy will do any work, since he was fired from his last job."

Jesse narrowed his eyes. He hated Cade Savage at that moment, but he loved his father more. He did not want trouble with the boss's son.

It would be useless to explain that his dad had not been fired, that the ranch owner had been a lousy businessman who'd refused to listen to advice from more experienced ranchers. He'd borrowed too much money from the bank then spent it foolishly. At the end, he couldn't take care of his ranch or feed his horses, and he lost the ranch to the bank and the horses to the SPCA. One day there was simply no job for Mark Alvarez or the other men who had worked there to go to in the morning.

Jesse bit down on his lower lip and turned toward the poster again.

"Don't worry about the rodeo, Alvarez," Cade continued. "You and your dad just keep mucking horse crap out of my dad's stalls and leave the rodeo to the people who've actually got the money to compete."

Jesse clenched his fists as the boys' laughter filled the hallway. His father didn't muck stalls, but that wouldn't matter to Cade.

He took a deep breath and started toward the gym. He was more than halfway down the hall when he heard Cade's voice again.

"Hey, Jesse! Just because you can't hang with the men doesn't mean you can't barrel race with the women. My mom's got a spare mare, I think. You know how to ride the barrels, don't you? Didn't your mom barrel race before she ran away and dumped—"

Jesse couldn't hear the rest of Cade's words over the roar of his own blood in his ears. His composure left him; he spun on his heel and sprinted toward Cade, and was on soon on top of him, pummeling him.

After the initial shock, Cade punched back, catching Jesse hard in the ribs. They rolled on the floor, grappling and punching. A ring of students formed around them as cries of "Fight! Fight!" brought kids running from all directions.

Within seconds, Mr. Maxwell, a seventh-grade social studies teacher, pushed through the students and pulled Jesse and Cade apart.

"What's going on here?" he demanded, holding each boy by his shirt collar. Jesse was breathing hard, and his nose was bleeding. Cade's left eye was beginning to swell, and his lower lip was split and bloody.

Mr. Maxwell marched the boys in front of him down to Principal Blake's office. Jesse hugged his right side; every

step and every breath caused pain so sharp he wondered
if a rib was broken.

CHAPTER 12

ONE HOUR LATER, BOTH BOYS SAT IN THE PRINCIPAL'S OFFICE next to their fathers.

"I want to make it clear that fighting will not be tolerated at this school," Mr. Blake said. "Cade, I've known you for years. What's gotten into you, son?"

"He hit me first," Cade mumbled.

Mr. Blake sighed and turned to Jesse.

"You're new here, Jesse, but I want you to understand I won't put up with this type of behavior. There are better ways to settle your differences."

"Yes, sir," Jesse said, "but he shouldn't have talked about my mother like that."

Mark spoke up.

"Jesse's a real good boy. This kind of thing's never happened before."

"Ah, well, boys will be boys," Big Bob said. "No real harm done. Let's just shake hands and forget about it."

Mr. Blake shook his head.

"I'm afraid it's not that simple, Mr. Savage. I have to suspend the boys. It's a first offense for Jesse, and the first for Cade in quite a few months, so I'll suspend them for only one day. Now, as you all live on a ranch, I'm sure you'll keep these boys busy—and unhappy enough that this behavior will not be repeated."

Big Bob nodded. "That will not be a problem. Guaranteed." He turned toward Jesse's father. "Mark, if it's all right with you, Cade will meet Jesse at six a.m. tomorrow at the stables. Ranch hands can always use the help."

"You can't be serious, Dad." Cade straightened up in his seat. "That's what we pay *them* to do. They work for us."

"They work for me, son, not you. You hear me?"

Cade fell back into his seat.

"Yes, sir," he grumbled.

Jesse could tell his dad was disappointed with him; Mark Alvarez hardly said a word as they drove home.

"I'm so sorry, Dad. I know I let you down. But if you'd heard what Cade said…"

Mark gripped the steering wheel.

"It's none of my business how someone else raises their child, but I do care about how *you* turn out. It's clear you and Cade don't get along, and no one, especially me, is saying you two have to be friends. But we've got a good thing going here, Jesse. Do you want to mess that up?"

"No," Jesse said thickly. Suddenly, he found it hard to talk. "He said things, Dad. He said things about you, and about Mom."

"Are those things true?"

"No, but…we've got a house now, Dad. Why wouldn't she want to come back? What happened that was so bad Mom won't come back to us? What did I do?"

Mark sighed. "Nothing. It's never been about what you did, Jesse. You've got to trust me on that. I wish to God I could make it right for you, son. But I can't. And I don't know if I ever can."

"Of course you can, Dad. All you have to do is call her up and tell her to come back. Why won't you do that? I didn't get to see her the whole time we lived in Montana, and she lived in Laramie. Five years, Dad. We're all in Wyoming now. She'd come, don't you think?"

"I can't speak for your mother, Jesse. The only thing I can say is that when she—"

"Yeah, I know, Dad," Jesse said sadly. "Next time she calls, I can tell her all about it."

CHAPTER 13

JESSE'S RIBS WERE SORE WHEN HE WOKE UP THE FOLLOWING morning, but he did his best not to think about it. He would not give Cade Savage the satisfaction of knowing he had actually hurt him. He finished his breakfast, cleared away the dishes, and left the house.

Cade and Big Bob were waiting at the large barn. Cade looked sullen; his left eye was a brilliant purple, and his bottom lip was noticeably swollen. Jesse couldn't help himself; he snorted in laughter.

Big Bob had a long list of chores he expected them to complete. He planned to make sure they did not enjoy their day off.

Cade groaned when Big Bob presented each of them a wheelbarrow and told them they would begin the day by mucking out every stall at Savage Ranch. Cade's eyes narrowed, and he mouthed a not-so-nice word at Jesse. Big Bob didn't notice.

The boys headed inside the largest barn. Cade flushed when the stable hands who usually did the mucking laughed as he pushed by with his wheelbarrow. Jesse, who knew the men by name, had no reputation as the boss's son to save, so he called out to the men as he followed Cade into the stable.

"Hey, Carl," he said. "Hey, Danny. What's up, Henry?"

"Why don't you two get into fights a little more often?" Henry laughed. "Sure is nice not to have to muck out all these stalls."

"My father doesn't pay you men to just stand around and talk," Cade snarled.

"He is today, little man," Henry answered with a wink.

"We'll leave you boys to it," Danny said. "Make sure you do a good job, now."

The three men grinned as they left the stable. Jesse grinned back; they were just teasing, and it didn't bother him.

But he could see it did bother Cade—a lot.

Cade took the pitchforks, shovel, and broom out of his wheelbarrow and threw them into the first stall in disgust. He glared at Jesse.

"You know this is all your fault, don't you? Do you know how many horses are on this ranch? How many stalls?"

"Actually, I do," Jesse said. "And I've only lived here a month. But I bet you don't, since the only stall you ever go into belongs to *your* horse. You don't even know the names of the men who work here."

"Why should I?"

"They do the work. They're the ones who make this place run smoothly."

Cade rolled his eyes. "Those men are just laborers—like your father."

"My father," Jesse said pointedly, "is the foreman."

"And my father owns this ranch and everything on it." Cade smirked.

"But here you are, mucking out stalls with me, the son of a foreman," Jesse said. "Yeah, your dad owns all this, but he also knows the first names of all the men who work here. He knows stuff about them, too. So does your mom."

"Least my mom lives with me."

Jesse froze. He knew Cade was trying to bait him into a response, maybe even another fight. He took a deep breath; two could play this game.

"Know who else I see around the stables?" Jesse asked. "Beau. I see Beau here all the time, talking to the men, just laughing, hanging out, and having a good time. They really like Beau, the men. They respect him."

Cade exploded. "You shut up about Beau, Jesse. You hear me?"

Jesse picked up his pitchfork and went into a stall.

"You don't talk about my mother; I won't talk about Beau."

For the next three hours, Jesse and Cade worked side-by-side without speaking. There was a rhythm to the work, as each stall was cleaned in the same way. The boys began by using a shavings pitchfork to pick up the horse droppings and put them into the wheelbarrow. Then they pushed them out of the stable to the manure pile, where the droppings were dumped.

Next, any dry bedding in the stall was pushed against the walls. Wet bedding remaining on the floor was removed with the pitchfork and dumped into the wheelbarrow. Jesse and Cade then swept the stall floor and used the shovel to remove any remaining manure or wet bedding. Another trip was made to the muckheap to dump the wet bedding before dry bedding was spread out across the stall.

It was hard, tedious work, but Jesse kept up a brisk pace to force Cade to do the same. To further annoy Cade, he whistled and sang throughout the morning. He was as sweaty and dirty as Cade, but the more cheerful he became, the more Cade glowered.

It was lunchtime when the boys finished cleaning all the stalls. Jesse was about to leave and grab a quick lunch at home when Ellie Savage appeared at the stable door.

"You boys look like you could use a break," she said. "I've got lunch laid out at the house."

"Great, Mom," Cade said. "Be back here in a half-hour, Alvarez."

"Where are your manners, Cade?" Ellie inquired sternly. "Lunch is for the both of you. Are you hungry, Jesse?"

"Yes, ma'am," Jesse said with a big grin.

CHAPTER 14

JESSE'S FIRST THOUGHT UPON SEEING THE SAVAGES' KITCHEN was that it was larger than the house he and his father lived in. It wasn't, of course, but with the beautiful granite counters, polished wood cabinets, and gleaming pots and pans, it felt like it. A blue-and-white gingham tablecloth covered an oak table in front of a large bow window that offered a view of the pastures and the mountains.

"Cade, show Jesse where he can wash up before you eat."

Cade nodded toward the kitchen door.

"There's a hose out back."

"Cade Savage!" Ellie snapped. "I will not put up with such rudeness from any son of mine. Jesse is a guest in this house. Do you understand?" She crossed her arms over her chest, waiting for an answer.

"I'm so sorry, Jesse " Cade said in a mild voice, a sickly-sweet smile plastered across his face. "That was rude of me. I'll show you where the bathroom is."

"Much better," Ellie said. She dropped her arms and turned to the fridge. Cade's face twisted into a sneer, and he glared at Jesse out of narrow slits of eyes.

Jesse rolled his own eyes as he got up to follow Cade out of the kitchen. Wow. His mom really bought that? He laughed to himself.

As he trailed after Cade, he was again stunned not only by the size of the Savage home but by its furnishings. He stopped to gaze at the great room—a huge open area of shining hardwood floors, Shoshone rugs, and floor-to-ceiling glass windows. A wide oak staircase with three separate landings led to the upper levels of the house. Couches in earthen colors of brick red and dark mustard yellow faced a stone fireplace that took up the greater part of one wall. Pieces of Native American and Western artwork adorned the walls and tabletops.

Jesse imagined the Savage family spending time in this room—Big Bob, Ellie, Beau, and Cade, all lounging in front of a roaring fire as snow fell outside the massive glass windows. He allowed his mind to drift, and the scene changed. In place of Ellie Savage, he saw his mom sitting on the couch in front of the fireplace. She was wrapped in a beautiful Shoshone blanket, sipping her favorite tea and watching him play on the floor with his dog. His dad, working on a computer at a nearby desk, looked over and smiled. Jesse's mom moved; she wanted to say something to him. She opened her mouth to speak—

"Get away from there!"

Get away from what, Mom?

Jesse squeezed his eyes shut and shook his head, trying to clear his confusion. Why did his mom sound so angry? He opened his eyes and saw that he was standing in front of the mustard-colored couch. How did he get there?

Cade was striding toward him.

"I said get away from there, Jesse." Cade demanded. "What are you doing?"

"I was just looking," Jesse said as the image he had conjured faded. "I like that…" He scanned the table tops. "That bronze Indian statue." His face flushed red. Cade wasn't completely clueless. Could he have guessed what he'd been thinking?

"Yeah, well, don't touch it," Cade ordered. "That's a Remington. Follow me; bathroom's down the hall. And don't dry your hands on my mom's guest towels. I'll get you one from the closet."

"Your mom invited me to lunch. I think that makes me a guest. And guests get to use the guest towels."

Cade darted down the hallway. He stopped in front of a closet, opened the door and pulled out a small blue hand towel, which he threw at Jesse.

"Use this," he commanded.

Jesse let the towel hit him in the chest and fall to the floor. He stepped over it and into the bathroom. He turned to face Cade.

"I'm closing the door now so I can have some privacy. After I finish you can come in and feel which towel is wet. Then you can burn it so no one in your family has to touch it after I did."

"You better not—"

Jesse slammed the door in Cade's face. Laughing, he put his ear up to the door and listened to Cade breathing heavily on the other side. *Towels*, he thought. *Who cares about towels?*

CHAPTER 15

AT THE TABLE, ELLIE PLACED A STONEWARE DISH IN FRONT of each boy.

"What would you like to drink, Jesse? You can use the water cooler next to the fridge if you'd like cold water. I've also got iced tea, lemonade, and soda."

"A Coke would be great, Mrs. Savage. Thanks."

Ellie pulled a Coke out of the fridge and popped the top. She poured the soda into a glass full of ice and placed it in front of him.

I wonder if Cade appreciates how well his mother treats him, Jesse thought.

"Okay, boys," Ellie continued, "nothing fancy here. I've got some nice ham sliced up for sandwiches. There's also some chicken salad I just made."

"I'll have ham, please," Jesse said.

"Me, too," said Cade. "Only, I want those two pieces on the top of the platter—the ones I saw this morning."

"What kind of bread would you like, Jesse? We've got white, wheat, rye, and hard rolls."

Why does one family have so many kinds of bread? Jesse wondered.

"Are you guys having a party?"

Cade burst out laughing. He stopped when he saw the look on his mother's face.

"How about a roll, Jesse? They're really fresh." She went back to the fridge and pulled out a head of lettuce, a tomato, mayonnaise, mustard, and a jar of dill pickles. "We've got potato salad or chips. Or I could make French fries."

"French fries!" Cade exclaimed. "Please make French fries, Mom." A smile replaced his sulky expression.

"French fries it is," Ellie laughed. "For dessert, we've got some of those yummy chocolate chip cookies I picked up from that new bakery."

"They *are* good, Mom," Cade said, "but they're not as good as the ones you make."

"Why, thank you, Cade, honey, that's sweet." Ellie bent over to hug her son. Cade looked directly at Jesse as he reached up to receive his mother's embrace.

He's rubbing it in, Jesse thought. *He's showing me I don't belong in this big house with the pretty mother and four kinds of bread.*

Jesse whistled all the way back down to the stables. Mrs. Savage and all that good food had just about made up for the fact that Cade had been sitting right across from him.

"That sure was a good lunch," he said.

"Yeah, well, don't think you'll be invited into my house every day—or even again," Cade said.

"I don't know. Your mom's real nice, and I think she likes me a lot."

Cade jumped in front of him and tried to stare him down, eyeball-to-eyeball.

"What's that supposed to mean?"

Jesse met the glare without moving an inch.

"That I think your mom's real nice."

He stepped around Cade and headed toward the big stable. Cade could fight, no doubt about that, but he wouldn't back down from him. Ever.

CHAPTER 16

THE AFTERNOON'S CHORES WEREN'T ANY EASIER THAN THE morning's had been. The boys cleaned tack and groomed horses. They wrapped the legs of some of the horses and cold-hosed the legs of others. They walked up and down hills checking the watering system. Big Bob's stable hands used horses, trucks, and even ATVs to get around the ranch. Jesse and Cade were not allowed any of those options.

Big Bob had saved the hardest chore for last. The boys climbed into the hayloft in the main stable. After opening a set of double wooden doors, they took turns throwing the heavy bales to the ground below. The bales then had to be loaded in the bed of a pickup truck for disbursement to the fields and other stables.

Cade grimaced and wiped the dirt and sweat from his brow.

"It'll take forever if we do it this way. I'll throw 'em out; you go down and load 'em in the truck."

"Yeah, whatever," Jesse said. He was exhausted and not about to argue against anything that would end this day, even if the idea came from Cade. He wearily climbed down from the hayloft and stepped out into the stable courtyard.

Whump! A heavy hay bale slammed onto the ground, narrowly missing him. Tired as he was, he about jumped out of his skin. He looked up to see Cade hanging out of the loft and laughing.

"Whoops…didn't see you, Alvarez. Good thing I missed you, huh? That could have been bad."

It was close to 7 p.m. before Jesse and Cade finished every task on their list.

"You've done good, boys. I'm proud of you," Big Bob said. "Now, shake hands, and let's put this behind us."

Jesse stuck his right hand out, but Cade kept his arms folded across his chest. Big Bob looked at his son sadly.

"There's all kinds of people in this world, Cade," he said. "Some that have a lot, and some that don't have much at all. Those who don't have are no less than those who do. I had nothing when I was your age—nothing at all. Do you understand that?"

"I guess so," Cade mumbled.

"You're lucky to be my son, getting the benefit of all my hard work. But you've got to prove yourself, just like Beau did. No one's going to respect you just because you're the son of Big Bob Savage. If anything, it's the opposite. Now, shake hands, and then get on in the house and get cleaned up. Your mom's got dinner for you. After that, I expect you to write a letter of apology to Principal Blake."

"Okay, Dad." Cade gave Jesse's hand a quick brush. He then made his way slowly home.

Jesse watched him and wondered if he looked as exhausted as Cade did. He sure felt like it. He still ached from the fight, and after working all day, he was beginning to hurt in places that had never hurt before.

"C'mon, Jesse, I'll walk you home," Big Bob threw an arm around his aching shoulders. "I've got something I want to show you."

"Me?"

"Yes, you," Big Bob said. "Let's go by the lower corral."

Jesse heard the sound of snorting as they rounded the corner of the stable to the corral. It was accompanied by the thud of hooves.

He was confused.

"A horse? You want to show me a horse?"

"Yep. Take a look at him. What do you think?"

Jesse squinted in the gathering twilight. He examined the beautiful little chestnut paint that was trotting along the corral rail. He was lean and muscular—a young horse, but intelligence shown in his brown eyes, and he had a proud set to his head.

"He's got nice conformation. Withers aren't too high—or too low. Nice neck and back length, no bow to the legs, pasterns and hooves look good."

"That's a fine eye you've got for horses, Jesse," Big Bob said.

"He's beautiful, Mr. Savage. How'd you get him?"

Big Bob rested both elbows on the top rail of the corral.

"Got him from the Bureau of Land Management. He got caught up in one of their mustang roundups. Strange, though, he's so different looking from anything else the BLM's been bringing in. Reminds me of the Indian ponies in the Westerns I used to watch as a kid."

"I know the BLM is part of the government," Jesse said. "And I know they take care of public lands out West so we can hunt, and fish, and camp. But why can't they just leave the wild horses alone?"

"The wild horses and mustangs that live on public lands don't have any natural predators," Big Bob said. "There's too many horses and not enough food. If the BLM didn't step in and manage the herds, many of the horses would starve."

Frowning, Jesse looked from Big Bob to the mustang. Big Bob read the question on his face.

"No, the BLM doesn't euthanize healthy horses, Jesse. They have roundups and adopt the horses out to people willing to train and ride them."

"You got him at a roundup?"

"Yes, my wife saw him in one of their pens and told me about him. She's always on the lookout for her next great barrel prospect."

Jesse shook his head. "This one…" He pointed at the mustang. "…won't ever barrel race—even for someone as nice as Mrs. Savage."

Big Bob smiled, flashing his white teeth in the fading light.

"I agree one-hundred percent with you, Jesse. That's why I took him and gave her that handsome palomino she's been working with. I have to admit, there's something about this one. I can't put my finger on it, but it's there."

"Well, thanks for showing him to me." Jesse never tired of looking at horses, but he was exhausted and could think of nothing but taking a hot shower and stretching out on his bed. Tomorrow was a school day, and no way would his father let him stay home just because he was sore from doing chores. Especially when those chores were given as a consequence for getting suspended.

Big Bob started to laugh, a low rumble coming out of his throat.

"I didn't bring you here just to show him to you, Jesse. I know you don't have a horse for the rodeo. I also know what Cade said to you. What do you think about this guy?"

"But he's still a little green, right?"

Big Bob nodded. "A little, but he's a good boy. I wouldn't let you near a dangerous horse. He's halter-trained and can be led. We've introduced him to a saddle and bridle. There's no buck in him. Finish him, and he's yours for the rodeo."

Jesse looked up at Big Bob, sure that at any minute the tall man would start laughing and say it was all a joke. Big Bob was quiet, though; he waited for Jesse's reply.

"Are you serious?" Jesse finally asked.

"I don't fool around when it comes to horses, Jesse. Thought you knew that about me by now."

"I have to ask my dad."

"Oh, I've already done that. Ran everything by him first. So, what do you say?"

"Yes! I say yes!"

"Jesse, Cade's no slouch. Not as a horseman and not as a competitor. I want you to know that. I'm not just bragging because he's my son. You take this on, I expect you to see it through."

"I don't mean any disrespect, Mr. Savage, but it's Cade who underestimates me."

"I hope not. That would be a very dangerous thing for him to do."

"Does Cade know?"

"Not yet, but he will soon."

"Tell him tonight," Jesse advised. "If he's feeling anything like I am, he'll be too tired to put up much of a fight."

CHAPTER 17

THE FOLLOWING MORNING, HE WOKE EARLY FOR SCHOOL. It took him almost five minutes to climb out of bed and walk across his room. Every muscle in his body was sore and screaming. He felt like an old man as he made his way slowly into the bathroom and turned on the shower.

He was used to hard work, but yesterday had been brutal. The only thing that made the pain bearable was the knowledge that Cade probably felt as horrible as he did. As the hot water poured over him and he began to feel a little better, he laughed, remembering how humiliated Cade had looked as he mucked out stalls and scooped horse poop into a wheelbarrow in front of his father's stable hands. He couldn't wait to tell Aaron.

"Let me get this straight," Aaron said as they walked into art class. "You got a horse because you got suspended?"

Jesse grabbed the supply box for his table.

"Not exactly. Mr. Savage has a paint mustang he got from a BLM roundup a while back. I'm going to work with him, use him in the rodeo."

"What does he look like?"

"Tobiano markings. More chestnut than white, with a narrow blaze. Real pretty."

"You know how to start a horse?"

"He's already started," Jesse said. "Been ridden a little bit, too." He watched Aaron open the supply box sitting on the table between them and rummage through the scissors, glue sticks, colored pencils, paints, and markers. "But I'm going to finish him. Been around it all my life. Helped my dad some, too."

Aaron pulled out strands of brightly colored yarn from the bottom of the box.

"Watching somebody train a horse doesn't make you an expert, Jesse."

"Big Bob wouldn't have given the mustang to me if he didn't think I could do it. Hey, how about Reuben? Could he come over this Saturday?"

"Maybe. I'll ask." Aaron's attention shifted to Mrs. Roberts, the art teacher. He slid the yarn across the table and covered it with his hand. When Mrs. Roberts turned her back to the class, he quickly slid the yarn into his pocket. "What?" he said when he noticed Jesse watching him.

Jesse said nothing.

What in the world is he going to use that junk for, he wondered.

CHAPTER 18

JESSE WAS UP WITH THE SUN ON SATURDAY MORNING. HE WAS excited at the thought of working with the mustang, but he also knew he couldn't shrug off his weekend chores.

Mark had insisted Big Bob assign Jesse weekend work around the ranch. Jesse was allowed free time for friends and homework, but Mark wanted his son to realize work was part of life. Big Bob had agreed, but he also insisted on paying Jesse, saying any man who did a fair day's work on his ranch should receive a fair day's pay. Jesse was just about finished with his Saturday chores when he saw Aaron.

"Hey!" he called from the hayloft. "Where's Reuben?"

"Might be over later. He's busy on another ranch. But I can help."

"No, you might get hurt."

"Well, can I watch?"

"Sit up on the fence and stay out of the way," Jesse ordered. "I'll be right down."

He pulled off his work gloves and shoved them into a back pocket before he climbed out of the hayloft.

Big Bob and Cade were already at the mustang's corral; the horse didn't seem as restless as the first time Jesse had seen him. He stood in a far corner of the enclosure, his hindquarters and tail against the fence rails, and watched the humans with curious eyes.

Aaron ran ahead of Jesse and jumped onto the bottom fence rail right next to Big Bob.

"Hey, Aaron," Big Bob said. "Been a while since I've seen you. How are your mother and father?"

"They're fine, Mr. Savage. Your mustang's a beaut. I was telling Jesse how Reuben could have trained him, no problem."

Cade rolled his eyes. "Do we really have to listen to this?"

Aaron's eyes narrowed. He jumped down off the fence and walked up to Cade.

"Reuben can gentle even the wildest, meanest horse. He's one of the best trainers in all of Wyoming." Aaron turned toward Big Bob. "Isn't that right, Mr. Savage?"

Big Bob nodded. "One of the best I've ever seen," he said.

"Ha!" Aaron said, pointing a finger at Cade. "Ha!"

"Yeah, whatever," Cade said.

Jesse knew that if Big Bob had not been there, Cade would have said a lot worse, or maybe even have done a lot worse, to Aaron. For now, Cade just turned to his father.

"Dad, can we go to Chandlers now and get my new boots? They close early on Saturday."

"Yeah, best we get going. " Big Bob pulled his truck keys out of his pocket and tossed them to Cade. "Go ahead and start the truck, buddy."

Cade caught the keys and ran for Big Bob's truck. This was no work truck; it was outfitted with all the personal luxuries you could imagine—leather seats, GPS, sunroof.

And those were just the things he could see when Cade opened the driver's door. He'd already heard Cade brag about the heated steering wheel and seats and the entertainment system.

"Chandlers, huh?" Aaron said as he watched Big Bob and Cade drive off. "Figures he gets his boots from Chandlers. They're the nicest boots around."

"So what?" Jesse said, lifting the latch that kept the corral gate closed. "Cade's a jerk. When he comes back, he'll still be a jerk. He'll just be a jerk in expensive boots."

The mustang shook his head as Jesse as he entered the corral.

"Hey, boy," Jesse called out, low and slow. "I'm just coming in to get acquainted. That's all. I'm going to come over and say hello."

The mustang pawed nervously at the ground, his ears pricked forward as Jesse approached.

"Too fast! Back up!" Aaron called from atop the corral fence rail. "Give him some space. He doesn't like you coming up on him like that."

"Thought I told you to stay out of the way," Jesse said without turning. "I can handle this." He backpedaled and grabbed the halter hanging on a corral fence post.

"Are you really gonna try and put a halter on him already?" Aaron asked. "He just met you. Maybe you're pushing him too fast."

"It's a breakaway halter," Jesse said. "If he goes a little nuts, he won't get hung up on anything."

CHAPTER 19

FOR THE NEXT TWO HOURS, JESSE TRIED AGAIN AND AGAIN to get close to the mustang. He held the halter out in one hand, trying to get close enough so the mustang could sniff it and find out that it—and he—was nothing to be scared of. Aaron sat patiently on the top rung of the corral.

"Want to know how Reuben would do it?" Aaron asked. "'Cause I can show you. I know all his tricks."

"No!" Jesse hissed through clenched teeth. He was beginning to feel irritated—and confused. He had always had a way with horses. They liked him—he was patient and kind. And this horse, he knew, had already been haltered. So why did the mustang seem so scared of him?

He didn't want to disappoint Big Bob—or his father. Mark Alvarez had been enormously proud of this trust Big Bob had placed in Jesse.

"Trust me, boy," Jesse called to the mustang, who was once again keeping his distance across the corral. "I would never hurt you."

Aaron jumped down into the corral.

"I know what Reuben would say. He'd tell you just to sit in there with him for a while. You're rushing things. Let him get used to you and see you're not a threat."

Jesse glared at him. He was sweaty and thirsty, and although what Aaron said made sense, he was not in the mood to allow him to be his co-trainer. He would prove to Big Bob he was good enough and man enough to finish this horse.

Out of the corner of his eye, he checked to make sure the mustang was both keeping its distance and hadn't turned around on him. A horse that turns and shows you his hind end might be ready to kick.

"Aaron, get out of here, now!"

"All right, all right." Aaron threw his arms up in surrender. "I'm just saying Reuben's got some good techniques." He scampered back on top of the fence. "I'm right here if you need me."

Morning turned into afternoon, with Jesse getting no closer to the mustang. Every time he approached, the horse wheeled and galloped to the opposite end of the corral. Frustrated, Jesse decided to take a break.

He left the corral for the hose inside the stable, grabbing a bucket as he walked. He took off his Stetson and ducked his head under the hose. The cold water instantly revived him, but he didn't linger. Water was valuable on the ranch, and he wouldn't waste it.

He stuck the hose inside the bucket to fill it so the mustang could drink. From inside the stable, he could see only half of the corral. Aaron wasn't on the fence.

Good, maybe he got bored and went home.

He finished filling the bucket and turned off the hose. As he made his way around the corner of the stable, the rest of the corral came into view. Aaron was standing dead center in the middle of it. The mustang, no longer in the far corner of the corral, couldn't have been more than three feet away from him.

Jesse dropped the water bucket. His heart was racing, and his breath came in sharp rasps, but he stepped slowly toward the corral. The mustang couldn't have been taller than fifteen hands, but he looked immense standing near the small boy. He had seen what a kicking or rearing horse could do to an adult. He knew Aaron wouldn't last a minute if the horse spooked or felt threatened.

"Aaron, back up. Back up slowly, and get on the fence. Get out of there right now!"

Aaron turned to face him.

"Why?"

It was then Jesse noticed the horse didn't look spooked or angry. In fact, he was standing with a back leg bent and his head low—the sign of a relaxed horse. Aaron reached up with both hands and brought the horse's head even closer to him. He kissed the mustang full on the nose and stroked his forehead. Jesse's gaze followed Aaron's hands; the mustang was wearing the halter.

"Aaron, did you put the halter on him?"

"Well, duh, he didn't put it on himself."

"How'd you get it on him?"

Aaron gave him a quizzical look.

"All these years you've been living on ranches, and you don't know how to put a halter on a horse?"

"That's not what I meant." Jesse took a step toward the corral gate. The mustang snorted and took a step backward. Jesse stood still. "I meant, how did you get a halter on him when I couldn't?"

Aaron grinned. "He likes me. Can't you see that? It's like Reuben says, you gotta respect them. And you gotta come to an understanding with them. Reuben says that's the problem with some trainers, 'specially white men who think they can break Indian horses."

"And just like that…" Jesse snapped his fingers. "…you two have an understanding?"

"Yes, " Aaron said, eye-to-eye with the mustang. "You can come in now, but be careful."

Jesse pushed the gate open. The slight squeak of the hinges drew the mustang's attention, and he flattened his ears as he saw Jesse approach. Jesse stopped and stood still again. The mustang had avoided him before, but he hadn't behaved aggressively. He'd seemed to be the gentle boy Big Bob said he was. What had Aaron done?

"I thought you said it was okay," Jesse said.

"It is," Aaron said. "Trust me."

This should be the other way around, Jesse thought. *I should be the one calling Aaron into the corral and telling him to be careful.*

Aaron tugged on the halter and got the mustang walking toward Jesse.

"I told him to trust you. I told him we're friends."

"He's a horse, Aaron. He'll learn to trust me because I'll treat him kindly, not because you tell him to."

"Okay, then." Aaron let go of the halter. The mustang took one look at Jesse, wheeled again and galloped to the far end of the corral. Aaron laughed. "He can't learn to trust you, Jesse, if he won't get near you."

"All right, all right, do it your way. Just get him back."

No doubt about it now, Aaron was calling the shots where the mustang was concerned.

Aaron held out his hand.

"Come to me, boy," he said.

Without a second's hesitation, the mustang trotted to Aaron and stuck his nose in Aaron's palm. Jesse could see the mustang's lips moving as he nuzzled the hand and wrist.

"Come meet him now, Jesse, before he changes his mind."

"Oh, sure," Jesse said, "let the horse think he's in charge. Did Reuben teach you that?"

Aaron looked Jesse right in the eye.

"It's not about being in charge. It's about respect."

It wasn't worth arguing about, Jesse decided. He'd read about the bond Indians shared with the horses and ponies they'd tamed and ridden across the plains. He knew horses were an important part of Indian history and culture.

But he also knew horses were herd animals that needed and respected a strong herd leader. Each horse knew his place in the herd. Humans who lived with and worked with horses had to be the herd leaders.

Jesse walked up to the mustang, fully expecting him to bolt and run. He didn't. Instead, he snorted and shook his head. He wasn't happy about being so close to Jesse, but he stayed alongside Aaron and allowed Jesse to stroke his neck.

"Now," Aaron said, taking the mustang by the halter and leading him to the side of the corral, "close your eyes, Jesse. We've got a real surprise for you."

"You're kidding."

"Just do it. And no peeking. Put your hands over your eyes."

Jesse sighed and closed his eyes. He hoped Big Bob and Cade were still miles away at Chandlers. At Aaron's command, he dropped his hands and opened his eyes.

Aaron was sitting on the mustang's back. Sitting and grinning ear-to-ear.

"Surprise!" he crowed. He clucked his tongue, and the horse began to walk.

Jesse was speechless. He could only watch as Aaron, without a bridle, bit, reins, or saddle, rode the mustang around the perimeter of the corral.

Trees shaded the far end of the corral, and as Jesse squinted to see Aaron and the horse in the shadows, his heart skipped a beat. Aaron, now barefoot, was clad in a tan deer-hide shirt and leggings. A feather jutted out of his now-shoulder-length hair. A red-and-white beaded headband was stretched across his forehead.

I've seen that headband, Jesse thought. *Where have I seen that before?*

As quickly as the vision came, it faded. Aaron rode out of the shadows and into the sunlight, and Jesse saw him once again in the torn blue jeans and dirty green T-shirt he had been wearing all morning.

"Are you okay, Jesse? You look liked you've seen something scary."

"I honestly don't know what I'm seeing," Jesse said. "I don't understand any of this."

"That's okay. We didn't think you would—not a first. But you will."

"We?"

"Me and Dreamcatcher."

"Who's Dreamcatcher?"

"The horse, duh!" Aaron leaned over to pet the mustang's neck. "That's his name. I knew it as soon as I saw him."

CHAPTER 20

JESSE TOLD NO ONE—NOT EVEN HIS FATHER—WHAT HAD HAP- pened in the corral with Aaron and the mustang. Working with the horse was a lot easier after that first day. As long as Aaron was in the corral with him, Jesse could do just about anything with the horse.

Aaron would stay long after Jesse had turned the mustang out into the pasture. As long as Big Bob let him, the boy would sit on the pasture fence and watch the horse.

Dreamcatcher never strayed far. He seemed to be listening, as he grazed, to every word Aaron said. If nobody said anything, Aaron stayed until dark, and Big Bob drove him home.

March turned into April, and April turned into May, and the weather warmed. Jesse continued to sit with Mike and Logan at lunch while Aaron sat alone, but after school each day and on weekends, Aaron helped Jesse with Dreamcatcher. Slowly, Dreamcatcher became comfortable with a saddle and bridle.

The only time Jesse saw Cade outside of school was when Cade and his friends would call out to him as they splashed in the Savage's in-ground pool.

"I'd invite you to swim, Jesse," Cade would yell, "but I don't want to take you away from your ranch chores."

"We'd feel really bad if your family lost the income," Luke added.

Jesse did his best to ignore Cade and keep his distance from him, so he knew something was up when he and Aaron arrived at the mustang's corral one Saturday and found Big Bob, Cade, and all of Cade's friends already there.

"You've done a great job with him, Jesse, you really have," said Big Bob.

"It was Aaron, mostly," Jesse said.

"Oh, I'm sure he was a big help." Big Bob ruffled Aaron's hair.

"No, you don't understand," Jesse began. "This horse—"

"Rodeo's coming up," Big Bob interrupted, "so, let's see how he runs. How about a friendly race here with Cade on Bandit?"

Jesse knew Big Bob wasn't really asking. If he wanted a race, it would happen. Still, Jesse didn't think it was a good idea. He wasn't even sure Dreamcatcher would let him on his back. Aaron had ridden him almost every day, but only recently had the mustang allowed Jesse to mount him.

"Mr. Savage, he hasn't been under saddle that long."

"Scared that me and Bandit will kick your butt?" Cade taunted.

"Not one little bit," Jesse said through clenched teeth.

"Relax, Jesse, this is just a test," Big Bob said. "We just want to get a time on him, see how he reacts to a little competition. It doesn't really matter who wins."

"Yeah, relax, Jesse," said Cade. "You don't want to be all tense when you're eating Bandit's dust."

Cade's friends fell over themselves laughing.

"Let's do this," Jesse said.

"That's the spirit." Big Bob clapped Jesse on the back. "Now, we need something to mark the finish line."

"How about Mom's practice barrels?" Cade offered. "There's two over in the schooling ring."

"No," said Big Bob, "definitely not. I made that mistake once, and let's just say the ensuing ruckus outweighed the convenience of the situation."

"Huh?" Cade looked up at his father.

"Never mind," Big Bob said. "You'll understand someday. We'll use a couple of feed buckets."

Dreamcatcher pinned his ears back as Jesse approached with his saddle pad, saddle, and bridle. The mustang skittered sideways, tossing his head.

"Aaron, maybe you should ride him. He's not going to let me get near enough to mount him."

"Sure he will," Aaron said. "Here, give me his bridle."

Aaron slipped the bit into Dreamcatcher's mouth and the bridle over his head. The fact that he had to stand on a mounting block to do this caused even more laughter from Cade and his friends. It didn't seem to bother Aaron, but as Jesse tightened the cinch on the saddle, he seethed quietly. Why did these guys always have to follow Cade's lead? Why did they think it was funny to torment Aaron?

Jesse held his breath, put his left foot in the stirrup, and hopped up into the saddle. Dreamcatcher snorted loudly and swished his tail. Jesse gathered the reins and circled Dreamcatcher around to face Big Bob, who was now standing about thirty yards away. The feed buckets had been set up to mark the finish line.

Aaron, Beau, and Cade's friends watched Jesse as he brought Dreamcatcher alongside Cade and Bandit. Big Bob held up a starting pistol. As the shot sounded, Cade and Bandit took off. Dreamcatcher backed up a few steps then reared and pawed the air.

"Settle him, Jesse," Big Bob called.

"I'm trying," Jesse said. But Dreamcatcher was fighting him. Jesse shifted his weight and tried giving the mustang more leg, but the horse wouldn't respond to anything he tried.

Aaron stepped up.

"It's okay, boy," he called.

The mustang, hearing Aaron's voice, whirled and whinnied as he searched for him.

"Go on, now, boy!" Aaron called again. "You take Jesse. It's okay. I promise, it's okay."

All of a sudden, Jesse felt the horse gather beneath him, felt the mustang's raw power and desire to run—just run. Like a flash, they were off.

Cade and Bandit were a good distance ahead of them, and the idea of losing to Cade Savage made Jesse feel sick. As if reading his mind, the mustang lengthened his stride, gaining on Cade with every powerful kick of his hooves. Soon, they were alongside Bandit. Cade looked over, his mouth forming a shocked O of surprise.

As they passed Cade and Bandit, Jesse had the sudden sensation he was flying. Savage Ranch faded away before his eyes; he was no longer racing Cade and Bandit but miles away in the wilds of the Wind River Mountains, surrounded by the thundering hooves of hundreds of mustangs. The saddle was gone, and he was riding bareback. The bridle was also gone, and he was holding not reins but the mustang's mane.

Jesse threw his arms straight up in the air as he rode in perfect balance with the mustang. He was a member of the wild herd, and he felt a surge of power and strength.

It took barely a minute for the vision to fade. He was back in the race. He understood the mustang more clearly now than he ever had before, and his heart broke as he realized what the horse had been forced to give up after he was caught and made to carry a man on his back.

The finish line came into view. Big Bob was whooping and jumping up and down like a kid. Beside him, Beau waved his hat and cheered Jesse on.

"Holy smokes!" cried Big Bob as Jesse flew across the finish line. "I can't believe what I just saw. Whoa! He's got some speed. And Jesse, that was some good riding!"

Jesse turned Dreamcatcher and trotted back to Big Bob.

"All I did was hang on," he admitted, sliding off the mustang's back. The horse was blowing hard and sweating. He needed to be cooled down.

Aaron grabbed the reins.

"I'll walk him," he said.

"Jesse's underestimating himself. Isn't that right, Cade?"

Cade had ridden well, but neither his father nor his brother had commented on that.

"Good race," he said sullenly.

"Time to give this guy a name, Jesse," Big Bob said. "He needs one if we want to enter him in the race. I've got to have something to put on the paperwork."

"How about Speed Demon?" Cade said.

"Oh! Oh! Chase the Wind," Luke suggested.

"Ride the Wind," Tyler said.

"No!" Aaron returned with the mustang. "*No!*"

"No to what, little man?" Big Bob asked.

"No to Speed Demon. No to Chase the Wind. No to Ride the Wind." Aaron's voice rose with each name. His face reddened.

"Dude, you're foaming at the mouth. Chill out, okay?" Luke said.

"He's got a name," Aaron said. "It's Dreamcatcher."

Cade, Luke, and Tyler howled with laughter.

"My little sister has a pony named Dreamcatcher," Luke said. "It's in one of her Pretty Pretty Pony playsets."

Aaron folded his arms tightly across his chest.

"We're not changing his name, Jesse."

"You know about this, Alvarez?" Cade smirked.

Big Bob shifted his gaze from Jesse to Aaron and back to Jesse again.

"It's your call, Jesse. You're the one who trained him, and you'll be the one who rides him."

Jesse knew he should say something. He owed Aaron so much for helping to train the mustang, but Cade and Luke were right. *Dreamcatcher* did sound like the name of a little girl's pony, one that would be tacked up with a pink saddle pad and have pink ribbons braided into its mane.

"I kind of like Speed Demon…"

Aaron dropped the mustang's reins and took off running.

CHAPTER 21

THE BOYS AT SCHOOL LOOKED AT JESSE A LITTLE DIFFERENTLY the next day. Word had spread about the race, about how Jesse Alvarez had beaten Cade Savage and Bandit. Even Lexi waved and smiled as Jesse walked by in the schoolyard. Behind her back, Jen caught Jesse's eye. She stuck her finger down her throat and pretended to throw up.

Jesse wanted to talk to Aaron and explain about the mustang's name. But when he had walked out on his front porch that morning, fully expecting to find Aaron sitting on the steps as usual, Aaron was not there.

He must really be mad at me, Jesse thought.

He sailed through his morning classes. At lunch, he noticed that the place where Aaron usually sat was empty. He sat with Logan and Mike, but a few boys from Cade's table came over to talk with him. During PE, he was chosen first for baseball. He would talk to Aaron tomorrow.

But Aaron didn't come to school the next day, or the next day, or the day after that. No one mentioned him. Jesse began to worry. Each morning that he found his porch steps empty, his worry intensified.

The longer Aaron was absent, the more restless the mustang grew. He stopped letting Jesse handle him, and he flattened his ears at anyone who tried to come near. If he wasn't standing with his head over the fence facing the mountains in the distance, he was walking endless circles around the corral's perimeter.

After four days of finding his front porch empty, Jesse decided to ask for help. He stayed in his seat as the kids in his math class filed out. Only when the room was empty did he approach Miss Miller's desk.

"Um...Miss Miller, do you know if everything is all right with Aaron?"

"Oh, Jesse, I wish I knew. I worry about Aaron. He's so...so..."

"Vulnerable?"

"Yes, Jesse, that's exactly right. Aaron is a vulnerable child in many ways. I can see you're worried about him, too."

"It's just that I...I think this is my fault," Jesse said. "See, there's this horse...he's not really mine, but Big Bob...I mean Mr. Savage...let me name him. Aaron, he's really great with the horse; they have this connection. An understanding. Anyway, Aaron wanted to name the horse Dreamcatcher. But I didn't like that name, and I said no. And Aaron hasn't been back to school since."

"Jesse, I'm not sure I understand that whole story, but this is in no way your fault. I want to make that very clear. I expect Aaron will be back to school soon. This isn't the first time he's been absent for multiple days."

"Okay, Miss Miller. Thanks." Jesse started for the classroom door.

"Wait." She motioned Jesse back to her desk. "I don't usually talk about my students' private lives, but I know you're Aaron's friend. I also know how much you mean to Aaron. He has a...difficult home life."

"Do you know where he lives? He never told me."

"He lives on the edge of the Wind River Reservation, at the very end of Boone Road."

"Do you think it would be okay if I went to visit him, just to see if he's all right? I could call first."

"There's no phone in the house, Jesse. That's what makes it so hard to know what's happening with Aaron when he doesn't come to school."

"Do you know the name of the ranch where his dad works? I could get my dad to drive me over there."

Miss Miller frowned. "Mr. Little Elk doesn't work on a ranch, Jesse. He salvages appliances and things people throw away. He repairs them and sells them."

"How about Reuben?"

"Who?"

"Reuben, Aaron's big brother. He'll know if anything's wrong with Aaron."

"Aaron told you about Reuben?"

"Yes. Reuben worked at Savage Ranch for Mr. Savage as a trainer. I'm not exactly sure why he left or where he works now. Aaron never said anything about that."

"Jesse," Miss Miller said softly, "Reuben's dead. He died over a year ago."

It took Jesse a minute to fully absorb his teacher's words.

"No, no. That can't be right. Aaron talks about him all the time. Reuben is everything to Aaron."

"I'm sorry, Jesse, very, very sorry. But it is true."

"How?"

"A friend of Reuben's from the reservation—someone he knew all his life—was high on meth, and he pulled a gun and tried to rob Reuben. Reuben tried to talk to his friend. He reached out for the gun. The boy panicked and shot Reuben in the stomach. He bled to death right there on the ground. I don't think the boy ever recognized him."

Jesse swallowed, felt a lump in his throat.

"Aaron didn't…he didn't see it?"

"He's the one who found Reuben."

Jesse's eyes swam. Feeling embarrassed by his tears, he turned away from Miss Miller. He didn't trust himself to speak. For a moment, the only sound in the room came from the ticking of the classroom clock.

Miss Miller broke the silence.

"Jesse? I'm going to give you Aaron's address and tell you how to get to his house. This is between us, I want you to understand. And…" She pulled a brown paper bag from behind her desk. "…would you give this to Aaron? It's full of clothes my son has outgrown."

"Yes, ma'am," Jesse said, reaching for the bag. "I'll be sure to do that."

CHAPTER 22

JESSE FLEW THROUGH HIS SATURDAY MORNING CHORES. HE then hopped on his bike and pedaled fast and hard down the long driveway that led out of Savage Ranch. Ellie Savage, in her big white SUV, passed him, coming into the ranch. She honked a hello and started to slow down, but Jesse waved and kept pedaling. He had caught a flash of blond hair in the passenger seat as he zoomed past the truck.

Although he wasn't sure whether it was Cade or Beau, he didn't want to waste time explaining where he was going in such a hurry. He shot out of the ranch gates onto the main road, checking to make sure he was heading south toward the reservation.

At school, he had learned that the Wind River Reservation was home to the Eastern Shoshone and Arapaho Indians; the two nations had shared its two million acres since 1928.

I'm sure glad Aaron lives on the edge of it, he thought.

He found Boone Road almost as soon as he pedaled onto reservation land. It was a dirt road, long and lonely. Out of breath, he stopped pedaling and coasted until he came to a small trailer home. The trailer had a truck hitch, but it obviously had not been moved in a long time, as it now rested on cinderblocks.

A clothesline, groaning under the weight of several pairs of men's jeans, was strung from the rear of the trailer to a low-hanging branch of a nearby tree. An old pickup truck sat on flattened tires behind the trailer. Appliances—ovens, washing machines, dryers, and microwaves that had obviously seen better days—littered the yard. Many of them lay in pieces.

Two scraggly adult dogs lay panting in the narrow shade provided by a rotted-out canoe. A small tan-and-black puppy tied to a lawnmower watched as Jesse balanced his bike on its kickstand.

Aaron sat on top of one of the broken washing machines. He was wearing the same dirty jeans and white T-shirt he'd had on the last time he'd been to school; Jesse recognized the stain on the T-shirt from when he had knocked his pint of chocolate milk off the cafeteria table and into his lap.

The patches on the knees of Aaron's jeans were beginning to curl up at the edges and pull away from the holes they were meant to cover. A sand-colored, too-big cowboy hat covered his head to below his ears. Jesse could just about make out his eyes below the brim after the boy tilted his head up.

Aaron didn't say a word as Jesse walked up to him. His face remained expressionless. Jesse felt uncomfortable with this silent Aaron.

"That your puppy?" he asked. "Why is she tied up like that?"

When Aaron finally spoke, he stared off into the distance instead of looking at Jesse.

"What if she ran off into the mountains and got lost? Poor little thing wouldn't last a day." He looked down and shook his head sadly. "Nope, not a day." He fell silent again.

Jesse cleared his throat.

"Miss Miller gave me this bag of clothes for—"

"Why did you come here?" Aaron interrupted.

"You haven't been in school. I wanted to see if you were all right."

"Why? It's not like we're friends."

"Well, we are."

"No, you said so yourself." Aaron slid off the washing machine. His sneakers, missing shoelaces, popped off of his feet. He shuffled back into them. "Remember when you ditched me to sit with Mike and Logan?"

"I said you weren't my *only* friend."

Aaron turned his back. He took the Stetson off and examined it closely before brushing the brim with a flick of his fingertips.

"I better put this back inside. Reuben will get real mad if he finds out I borrowed it again without asking."

"I know about Reuben," Jesse said.

Aaron froze.

"Know what?"

"I was worried about you. I went to Miss Miller."

"Miss Miller shouldn't be telling other people's business," Aaron said.

"Everyone at school knew. Everyone but me."

"So?"

"So, why didn't you tell me? Why do you talk like he's still alive? People will think you're...You're…"

"Weird? Stupid? They already think that."

Aaron walked to the puppy and untied her. He hoisted her up to his shoulder, crooning softly into her ear as she covered his face with sloppy kisses. He started toward the trailer.

"Are you coming in?" he asked.

The trailer was clean but cramped. It had one large living room/dining room/kitchen area instead of separate rooms. A worn couch covered with a bright Shoshone blanket sat opposite a small television. A jelly jar vase holding plastic flowers sat on the small dining room table. Flower-print curtains covered the windows.

Aaron filled a small dish with water for the puppy.

"Where's your mom?" Jesse asked.

"Hospital," Aaron said. "Sometimes she eats the wrong food, and her diabetes acts up real bad."

"How does she know if it's the wrong food?"

"I don't know. Reuben used to help her. He read the labels on cans and stuff."

The puppy finished lapping the water and tottered toward Aaron. She yawned, plopped down on a section of the faded carpet, and began licking her front paws. Aaron scooped her up and started down a narrow back hallway.

"C'mon." He gestured for Jesse to follow him.

CHAPTER 23

AARON'S BEDROOM WAS THE SIZE OF A LARGE CLOSET. IT HELD a bed, a small dresser, and a lamp with a bucking bronc shade. It was the dreamcatchers that caught Jesse's attention. They were everywhere—suspended from the ceiling, covering the walls, taped to the closet door.

He reached up to touch one.

"Whoa, where'd you get these?"

"Made 'em. Just like the ones I gave you." Still holding onto the puppy, Aaron launched himself onto the bed. A cacophony of twangy noise issued from the springs as the mattress, with its single sheet and dingy-white blanket, sagged in the middle even under Aaron's slight weight. He picked at something in the puppy's fur.

"Darn," he said, "another flea."

"I always thought dreamcatchers were a Chippewa tradition."

"They are," Aaron said. "But lots of nations make them. The Chippewa hung them over their children's beds to protect them from nightmares. Bad dreams get caught in the dreamcatcher's net, but the good dreams slide down the feathers to the sleeping person."

"What do you use to make them?"

"Willow tree branches are the best because you can bend them into a circle, and they won't break. The Chippewa used animal tendons for the net, but I use string."

"And the yarn from school?" Jesse asked.

Aaron sat straight up.

"That stuff was going to be thrown out! It was scraps... end pieces."

"I know," Jesse said. "I just wondered why you wanted it."

Aaron pointed to his closet.

"That one over there has pieces of the blue ribbon Reuben won for a science fair project. And that one..." He pointed to the large dreamcatcher at the window. "...has the buttons from his favorite shirt."

"They're cool. Are you going to sell them?"

"No," Aaron said quietly, "that's not why I made them." He gently placed the now-sleeping puppy in the center of his pillow. "There," he whispered, "all comfy now."

He stroked the puppy's head and back. She sighed and started snoring.

Aaron slid off his bed and went to the window where the largest dreamcatcher hung from a bent curtain rod. Bits of leather attached Reuben's metal buttons to the dreamcatcher's net, and they shone as they caught the rays of the afternoon sun.

"I dream about Reuben all the time," he said.

"You dream about him because you miss him, Aaron. That's normal."

"You don't understand, Jesse."

Aaron leaned forward until his forehead touched the windowpane. He gave the large dreamcatcher a gentle push. As it began to spin and sway, Reuben's metal shirt buttons reflected the sun and little dots of light danced around the room.

"For a long time, all I dreamed about was finding Reuben that day, finding him bloody and cold, a big hole where his stomach was."

Aaron's bedroom now felt even smaller to Jesse. He didn't know what to say. He wished his dad were here—or even Big Bob. They might know how to comfort Aaron.

Aaron turned to face him.

"So, I made the dreamcatchers."

Jesse pointed around the room.

"Each one of these has a bad dream about Reuben caught in its net?"

"They're supposed to," Aaron said. "Dreamcatchers are supposed to catch the bad dreams before they get to you. Only good dreams are supposed to get through. But mine weren't working. No matter how many dreamcatchers I made, none of them kept the bad dreams about Reuben away."

"Maybe you should talk to someone, Aaron. About so many bad dreams. Someone at school, like Miss Miller, or… what's the guidance counselor's name? Mr. Demas. I could talk to him first—explain things."

Aaron shook his head. "I don't need to do that, Jesse. Not now, not now that the mustang has come."

"The mustang? What's he got to do with any of this?"

"When he came to Savage Ranch, the dreamcatchers starting working the way they should," Aaron said. "The bad dreams about Reuben stopped. A good dream got through."

"What happened in the dream?"

Aaron's face lit up.

"Reuben came to me. I knew he wouldn't leave me forever. He was riding the mustang, riding Dreamcatcher. Don't you see what the mustang is?"

Jesse ran his fingers through his hair.

"No, I guess I don't."

"He *is* the dreamcatcher. He caught Reuben's spirit and brought it to me in a good dream. The mustang brings

Reuben to me almost every night now. I reckon Reuben's spirit gets stronger each time I have that dream. So, now I make dreamcatchers to hold Reuben's spirit. When I've made enough, I reckon the mustang will bring Reuben back to me for real. That's why his name is so important."

"Aaron, dead people don't come back. And the mustang...well, he's not leaving Savage Ranch each night to see you in a dream. Do you really think Reuben's in these little pieces of yarn and string you took out of Mrs. Roberts' art boxes?"

"Dreams are powerful, Jesse—magic. The Shoshone know that. I wouldn't expect you to understand."

"The mustang's not yours, Aaron."

"He's not Mr. Savage's, either."

"What's that supposed to mean?"

Aaron lowered his eyes and looked away. His secretiveness surprised Jesse. He had never had to prod Aaron to share his thoughts or say what he was thinking before; most of the time, it was impossible to get Aaron to *stop* talking.

"The horse hasn't been right since you left," Jesse said. "I can't ride him anymore. No one can. We can't even get near him. He just stands at the fence all day...waiting. It's like he's waiting for you."

"He *is* waiting for me."

"You've got to come back, then. I still don't understand why you haven't been to school. You don't look sick."

"School?" Aaron frowned. "Jesse, haven't you been listening? I'm in the middle of something important."

"I don't understand," Jesse said.

Aaron lay back down on the bed, curling his body around the sleeping puppy. Dirt from the bottom of his sneakers crumbled onto the sheets and blanket. "Come back tomorrow, and I'll explain everything," he said.

"I promised Mike I'd go over to his house," Jesse said, feeling immediately guilty as he watched Aaron's face crumple with disappointment. "But I'll see you at school on Monday, right?"

"Sure," Aaron said. "See you on Monday."

CHAPTER 24

THE NEXT DAY, JESSE WENT TO MIKE'S HOUSE. THEY PLAYED video games and ate pizza. Around 3 p.m., Mike's dad drove him home. He had to read three chapters of a novel for Language Arts and study for an American history test.

"Hey, Dad, I'm home," he called, slamming the door behind him.

Big Bob was sitting in the living room with Jesse's dad. Neither man looked happy.

Mark Alvarez stood and came toward his son.

"Jesse, did you go out to the reservation to see Aaron yesterday?"

Jesse nodded. "Yesterday morning. I rode my bike."

"His father came to see me today," Big Bob told him. "Aaron's missing."

A terrible feeling took hold of him. His stomach lurched, and he felt his heartbeat start to hammer in his chest.

"What? Is he hurt? Did someone take him?"

Big Bob got up and leaned on the fireplace mantle.

"Mr. Little Elk came home from the hospital yester-day afternoon after visiting Aaron's mom. He and Aaron had dinner. Then Mr. Little Elk went back to the hospital. Aaron was watching TV with his puppy. When his dad came home around eight-thirty, Aaron was gone."

"Did his dad call the police?" Jesse asked.

"Yes, but it took him some time. He had to drive to a neighbor's house to use a phone, " Mark said. "They've been out all night."

"There's just no sign of him," Big Bob said.

"Did Aaron leave a letter or a note saying where he was going?" Jesse asked.

Mark shook his head. "He left something, but it's not a note. It's there, on the kitchen table. Your name's on it, Jesse."

"The police brought it over," Big Bob said. "They had to open it. They're thinking it might be some kind of clue, and that you might know what it means."

Jesse walked into the kitchen. Aaron had taped newspaper around the gift, maybe trying to keep it private. But the tape had been peeled back and many of the newspaper pages were torn. Jesse saw feathers and a glint of silver peeking out from the newspaper and knew right away what Aaron had left for him.

"Why would Aaron want you to have that?" his dad asked.

"I have no idea. I really don't. This is special to Aaron. He made it out of stuff that belonged to Reuben. It was hanging at his window yesterday. Aaron has some weird idea about dreamcatchers and his brother. And the mustang's part of it."

"The mustang is missing, too," Big Bob said.

Jesse stood silently, remembering what Aaron had said about the mustang not belonging to Big Bob.

"It had to be Aaron that took the horse," Big Bob said. "They both went missing the same day. But that mustang has turned into such a maniac. How did that little boy manage to get him off of the ranch without anyone seeing or hearing him?"

"That mustang loves Aaron," Jesse said. "He'd go anywhere with him." He stared at the message Aaron had written on the newspaper: *I don't need this anymore.* Did Aaron really think the mustang could bring his dead brother back to him?

He held the dreamcatcher up with one hand so that its feathers brushed the palm of his other hand. Reuben's silver shirt buttons flashed in the glow of the kitchen light. He felt the hairs on the back of his neck and on his arms stand up, a spooky feeling that made him shiver.

CHAPTER 25

JESSE CLOSED HIS HISTORY BOOK AND PUSHED IT AWAY. HE reached across the desk and turned off the small study lamp. Leaning back in his chair, he sat in the darkness staring out the window. He took a deep breath, rubbed his eyes, and exhaled loudly; so much for George Washington, the American Revolution, and tomorrow's history test.

His thoughts kept wandering to Aaron and the mustang, to his conversation with his dad and Big Bob. He'd placed the new dreamcatcher on the top shelf of his closet and slid the door shut.

He sat for a while before changing into the T-shirt and shorts he slept in. He stretched out on his bed with his history book but was soon fast asleep.

He woke to the sound of soft but persistent knocking on his bedroom window. The clock read four a.m. He pushed out of bed and drew the curtains aside.

Cade Savage stood on the other side of the window, fully dressed and with Bandit behind him. Instantly alert, Jesse unlocked the window and pushed it up.

"What do you want?" he demanded.

"Get dressed," Cade said. "Saddle Joker. He's in the third stall in the back stable."

"I know where Joker is!" Jesse said. "Why are you here?"

"We're going to find Aaron and bring him and the mustang home."

"You're kidding me, right?" Jesse said. "Why do you even care? You and those jerks you call friends make fun of Aaron any chance you get."

"Do you want to find him or not?" Cade gathered Bandit's reins and turned the horse to lead him toward the woods. "I'll wait for you where the stream makes its first bend."

"You really think I'm going anywhere with you?"

"Dress warm. Pack a bedroll."

"Bedroll? What is this—a camping trip?"

"He's gone up into the mountains. I know he has. And stop yelling—you'll wake your father."

"What am I supposed to tell him?"

"Tell him the truth. I did."

"Your father knows about this?"

"He will when he wakes up tomorrow. I left him a note on the kitchen table. You should do the same."

"That's why you're sneaking out in the middle of the night?"

"Of course. He would have said no if I'd asked. Your father probably would, too."

"Got that right," Jesse said. "This is stupid, sneaking off."

"Either get dressed and meet me down by the stream, or get back in bed," Cade answered. "I'll wait fifteen minutes, and then I'll head out on my own. Should be enough time, seeing as you're such a genius with horses and all."

Jesse thought he saw a flash of a smile on Cade's face just before he disappeared in the darkness of the night.

He flew around his bedroom, shedding his shorts and tugging on underwear and a pair of jeans.

This is crazy, this is crazy, he thought, buckling his belt and pulling a T-shirt over his head. *I don't like Cade Savage; he's the biggest butthead I've ever met. I'm supposed to believe that, all of a sudden, he's turned into a nice guy?*

He buttoned a flannel shirt over the T-shirt, and over that he zipped up a jacket. Cade was right; it would be cold up in the mountains, even in May.

He turned the doorknob slowly and crept out of his bedroom, carrying his socks and boots. He didn't want to risk waking his father. He found a scrap of paper and a pencil and scribbled a quick note: *Dad – Went with Cade to find Aaron. Don't worry, Jesse.*

As quietly as he could, he grabbed a package of hotdogs, five small bags of Doritos, a box of cookies, and a few apples and shoved them into his backpack. He put his hat on, walked on tiptoe to the front door, and stepped out into the cool night air.

After pulling on his socks and boots, Jesse raced across the ranch, keeping to the path behind the hands' cabins and bunkhouse just in case someone was awake. He was breathing hard by the time he entered the back barn. Leaning against the front of Joker's stall, he filled his lungs with huge gulps of air while the dark bay nickered softly at him.

Jesse turned to stroke the gelding's neck.

"Are you laughing at me?" he whispered. "I'm a funny sight, huh, boy?"

Joker tossed his head as if nodding in agreement.

"You understand me, boy, don't you," he continued to whisper. "I know you do."

He haltered Joker and led him out into the long aisle running the length of the stable; the echo of the horse's hooves made the space seem cavernous. He could hear soft snorting and movement in the blackness of the stalls they passed. One by one, the elegant heads of Joker's curious barn mates began to appear over the stall doors.

"If anybody asks, you didn't see a thing," Jesse whispered.

He put Joker into the cross ties.

"I'm sorry about this, boy. Sorry about making you get up so early and leave your nice warm stall."

The gelding's ears swiveled forward in mild interest. He didn't seem at all upset.

Jesse worked quickly, using a currycomb and brush to groom Joker. Fifteen minutes or not, he would not saddle any horse without grooming at least his saddle area and checking his hooves to see if they needed to be picked.

"Cade's not going anywhere without me, boy," He said. "He needs my help."

He knew exactly where Joker's bridle and saddle were in the tack room, so he didn't need to turn the light on and advertise to the ranch's early risers what he was doing. He also knew his own father would be getting up soon, so he worked quickly. He placed a saddle blanket on Joker's back then hefted the saddle up and over the horse. He cinched it quickly but carefully. Then he undid the cross ties and slid the bridle over Joker's nose and head as he slipped off the halter. Joker took the bit without any fuss.

"Good boy," Jesse said again. He attached his bedroll to the back of the saddle with thin leather straps, gathered Joker's reins and clucked softly at him. "C'mon, boy, let's go."

He led the quarter horse out of the barn to the edge of the woods. Like Cade, he would also walk his horse to the stream instead of riding him there. Horses didn't see as well at night as people did. It was still dark, and Joker might stumble.

CHAPTER 26

NIGHT WAS FADING FAST BY THE TIME JESSE FOUND CADE AT the stream. The peaks of the Wind River Mountains, softened by the early morning sun, were slowly becoming visible against an emerging blue horizon.

"Daylight's coming." Cade mounted and gathered his reins. "We better get going."

"I'm not going anywhere until you explain this to me," Jesse said, "because I don't believe you give a damn about Aaron."

"You don't know anything about me."

"I know enough to believe there's got to be something in this for you. You'll never convince me you're doing this for Aaron's sake."

Cade turned Bandit's head and started in the direction of the mountains.

"Either mount up and ride out with me or go home and get back in bed," he called over his shoulder.

"What makes you even think you know where Aaron is? The Wind River Range is huge. We could look for weeks and not find him."

Cade swung Bandit around to face Jesse.

"There's a place Reuben took Aaron to all the time. A few hours beyond the foothills near Crowheart. They used to go fishing in Red Canyon. Aaron did a report about it in school. I think he would go there because it's the place that most reminds him of happy times with his brother."

Jesse hated to admit it, but Cade could be right.

"Did you tell your dad?"

"Yes. And my mom. And Beau. And you know what? They didn't listen to me. Like always. The police are looking for Aaron in town, in other Shoshone homes, near the school—in all the wrong places. Decide now, Jesse. Come with me to find Aaron or go home. I'm not wasting any more time."

Jesse swung up into the saddle. He didn't trust Cade one little bit, but the thought of Aaron somewhere up in the mountains by himself bothered him more.

I should have gone back to Aaron's instead of going to Mike's house, he thought. *Maybe Aaron wouldn't be missing now if I had.*

They rode without talking. Jesse knew his dad was up by now. A wave of guilt washed over him as he realized how scared his father would feel reading his note alone in the kitchen.

The crags of the Wind River range loomed closer. Soon, Jesse and Cade were at the foothills, starting the slow climb up into the mountains. It was unfamiliar territory to both boys, so they picked their way around the tall trees and through the brush and scrub very carefully.

They rode single file along a narrow rock ridge overlooking a deep gorge. Jesse watched a black bear wade into the clear mountain stream that cut through the bottom of the gorge. The bear made a quick movement with one huge paw, and a fish flipped up into the air. He smiled as the bear lunged forward and snagged the fish out of mid-air with a snap of its jaws. He easily imagined wild mustangs living up here.

Their pace remained slow and steady as the trail took them down into the gorge. Jesse craned his neck, squinting as he scanned the red rock formations above him. A strange feeling came over him, nervousness that started in the pit of his stomach and grew. The hairs on the back of his neck stood up, and he had the sensation he was being watched. He squirmed in his saddle.

"Cade, does anyone live up here? Anyone from the reservation?"

"I don't know where those people live."

Something's out of place, Jesse thought. He squeezed the reins; Joker stopped.

And then he saw him—halfway up the side of the gorge, standing on a ledge. How the heck did he manage to get up there?

Cade looked over his shoulder and stopped.

"What now?" His irritation showed in his voice. He followed Jesse's gaze up the side of the mountain and saw the stranger. "Hey! Hey, you!" His voice echoed throughout the gorge.

The figure remained still and quiet. He looked down from his rocky perch with an unflinching gaze that made Jesse's nerve endings tingle.

Cade started to laugh.

"What is this, rock-climbing day on the rez? Real smart. I'm talking to you!" He tried again. "I know you hear me!"

"I've seen him before, on my first day at the ranch," Jesse said. "I thought he was one of your dad's ranch hands."

"Sure, Alvarez. You recognize him from down here? I don't believe that. I can't even see his face."

"It's the beaded headband," Jesse said. "I remember it."

Cade twisted in his saddle to face Jesse.

"How many Indians around here do you think wear headbands?"

"A lot," Jesse said, "but I've never seen another like this one. It has red and white beads in some pretty crazy patterns."

Cade stared at him.

"Real funny, Alvarez," he finally said as he kicked Bandit with his heels.

Drifting clouds parked in front of the sun; a shadow passed across the face of the gorge. When the sun finally emerged and shafts of golden light once again illuminated the cliff, the rock ledge was empty.

"Let's go, Joker." Jesse squeezed with his legs. Maybe it wasn't a good idea to ride too far away from Cade right now.

By mid-morning, his stomach was grumbling, so he reached back to a saddlebag and brought out a bag of Doritos. The bag's crinkling broke the stillness of the morning.

Bandit laid his ears back and jigged sideways. Glaring at Jesse, Cade gathered his reins, steadied the horse, and got him moving forward on the trail again.

"You're spooking Bandit," he hissed.

"'I'm hungry," Jesse mumbled, his mouth full of Doritos. "I might even need to eat another bag. I could share some with Bandit; Joker loves Doritos."

Cade responded by squeezing his legs into Bandit's sides and galloping away.

Jesse shrugged.

"More for us, Joker."

He saw no reason to pick up his pace just to stay with Cade. He kept his eyes and ears open for any sign of Aaron, assuming Cade was doing the same.

He caught up to Cade in the late afternoon as they crested a wide, high butte. He stopped Joker alongside Bandit and took in the view.

A valley spread out below, meadows full of nothing but green grass, cedar trees, wildflowers, and mule deer. A single hawk floated gracefully overhead, carefully scanning the ground. It suddenly folded its wings and dove like a missile toward the floor of the valley, where it scooped up something small and furry. Jesse heard the victim's squeaks of protest as the hawk rose into the sky and soared away.

More mountains stood on the other side of the valley. By now, the boys were miles from Savage Ranch, miles from human habitation of any kind. Behind them, a coyote broke from a cover of low brush in pursuit of a quail it had flushed out of the sage.

Jesse rested his hands on Joker's withers. He took a deep breath and exhaled slowly.

"Where are you, Aaron?"

"We're getting close to the canyon," Cade answered. They were the first words the boys had spoken to each other in hours.

They stopped for the night, taking care of Joker and Bandit before they even thought of doing anything for themselves. They took off the horses' bridles and saddles, brushed them, and took them to a nearby stream for water. Cade ran a rope between two trees and picketed them, leaving enough room they could move and graze. The boys then spread out their blankets and sleeping bags.

"I brought a tent, but I guess we don't need it," Cade said.

"Nah," Jesse agreed. "It's going to be a clear night."

As darkness fell and the air became cooler, Jesse built a fire with kindling and fallen tree branches. He took out his pocketknife and sharpened the ends of two sticks. Cade sat down on his sleeping bag and pulled off his boots with a loud sigh.

"Hungry?" Jesse asked. He pulled a package of hot dogs out of his saddlebag and sliced the plastic open.

"Yeah," Cade said. "I've got a couple bottles of water in my bag."

They speared the hot dogs with the sharpened sticks and roasted them over the fire. Between the two of them, they ate the entire package.

"Got any Doritos left?" Cade asked.

"Yeah, I've got some apples and cookies, too. Do you have another bottle of water?"

After eating and checking on Joker, Jesse took his boots off and lay down on his sleeping bag. He bent his arms up behind his head.

The night sky, alive with thousands of bright, twinkling stars and a full moon, was visible through the canopy of trees.

Cade was awake, but Jesse didn't attempt to talk to him. He yawned, closed his eyes, and had begun to drift off when a tree branch suddenly snapped. His eyes flew open. Another branch snapped. Loudly. And then another, even louder.

Jesse bolted up. The dying fire was still strong enough to cast a faint, dancing glow on the nearby trees. All was darkness beyond.

"Who's there?" he called. He could hear the fear in his voice.

Cade rolled over onto his side to face Jesse.

"It's probably just a deer or something," he said. "Don't be such a wuss, Alvarez."

Jesse lay back down, his heart thumping. It took a few minutes before he felt calm. As the fire died and the night air grew even cooler, he began to shiver, although he still wore his jacket. He climbed inside his sleeping bag. Fatigue caught up with him, his body relaxed, and his eyes grew too heavy to keep open.

CHAPTER 27

SOMETIME DURING THE NIGHT, JESSE WOKE.

The cold, hard ground was uncomfortable. The fire's embers still glowed, but they gave off little heat. He pulled the sleeping bag over his head and curled up. He'd begun to drift off again when he heard soft footsteps behind him.

Across the clearing, the horses stirred. A flash of light sent a wave of warmth through the sleeping bag. The sound of loud crackling followed. Jesse turned toward the newly stoked campfire, grateful for the warmth.

He woke the next morning as the rising sun was just beginning to bruise the sky with swirls of pink and blue. Cade pulled granola bars and small packs of doughnuts out of his saddlebag.

"Here." He threw Jesse a pack of each. They ate as they saddled the horses.

Jesse stretched his hands up above his head.

"Man, my back is sore. Guess it would have been worse if you hadn't thrown those branches on the fire."

"What are you talking about? I didn't throw anything on the fire."

Jesse dropped his arms to his sides and stared at Cade.

"I heard you. The fire was about dead, then I heard footsteps, and all of a sudden the fire blazed."

"You were dreaming, Alvarez. I slept through the night. Some people can handle being outdoors, and some can't."

Nervousness returned to the pit of Jesse's stomach.

"Someone's following us," he said.

Cade laughed. "Sure they are. Real scary guy, building our fire up like that and making us all warm."

Jesse shook his head. "I know what I heard. I wasn't dreaming."

Cade stood over the remains of the campfire.

"There's two sets of boot prints here—yours and mine. What'd your guy do, fly around the campsite?"

"That man at the gorge," Jesse said. "It has to be him. We haven't seen anyone else for miles."

Cade popped another doughnut in his mouth and chewed quickly.

"Oh, right, the guy you've been seeing around the ranch."

"Maybe we need help," Jesse said. "No matter how much we want to find Aaron ourselves. There are people who do this kind of thing—rescue organizations with volunteers, people with helicopters."

Cade wiped powdered sugar on his jeans.

"I don't like you, but I didn't figure you for a coward."

It was Jesse's turn to laugh.

"I couldn't care less about what you think of me. You can keep playing this game, the one where you pretend to care about what happens to Aaron, but when this is over you'll go back to treating Aaron like dirt. You know it, and I know it. I also know why you're out here, and it's got nothing to do with Aaron."

Cade stopped eating, one hand holding half a doughnut stopped midway to his mouth.

"And what's that, Jesse?" he asked coldly. "The reason I'm here, I mean. Why don't you tell me?"

Jesse dropped Joker's reins, ground-tying him.

"You're doing this so you can prove to your dad that you're as good as Beau. Beau gave up his rodeo career for your dad and the ranch. How could you ever top that? You want to bring the mustang back. Admit it."

"Wow, what insight, Jesse," Cade said sarcastically. "You think about me that much? I never realized how much you cared."

"This isn't some buddy-buddy trip where we find how much we've got in common and start liking each other," Jesse continued. "I read too many of those sickening stories in school."

"Awww." Cade laughed. "I was so counting on you becoming my new best friend. Our families could do stuff together. Our moms could go shopping…oh, wait…"

"Why don't you shut up!" Jesse shouted.

"Why don't you make me?" Cade returned.

Jesse walked toward him.

"You sure you want me to do that? Mr. Maxwell's not here to break us up."

The boys were now inches from each other, staring eye-to-eye and standing toe-to-toe.

Cade backed off first; he shook his head and turned his back to Jesse.

"I'm not doing this now." He picked up his hat and swiped it against his leg to shake off dirt. "You want to come with me, come with me. You want to go home, go home. Makes no difference to me. I'm going on to the canyon."

Jesse swore to himself. He had little choice but to follow Cade. He had no idea where he was or how to get back down the mountain to Savage Ranch.

The day grew cold and gray, and after a few hours on the trail, a steady drizzle descended on them. Jesse's mood grew as cloudy as the day. He tried to fight off the dreary feelings, but the farther he and Cade traveled, the gloomier he felt. Being soaked to the bone in wet clothes didn't help.

It was easy to lose track of time when there was no sun. Guessing it was late afternoon, he suggested they stop and rest the horses. Cade grunted in agreement. The steady rain had dampened his mood, too, despite the fact he wore a waterproof oilskin jacket and hat.

Jesse dismounted and started to rummage through his saddlebags for something to eat. He found one last bag of Doritos crumpled at the bottom of the saddlebag.

"Yes!" he exclaimed. He ripped open the bag and started crunching on the chips.

Cade shot him a sour look.

"You're doing that on purpose, aren't you, Alvarez? Just so you can spook Bandit again."

Jesse tilted the bag up so he could catch the last few broken chips directly in his mouth. He wiped the red spice crumbs from his hand on the back pocket of his jeans before crumpling the bag loudly. If he had been in a better mood, he might have given Cade an answer that would have derailed the fight he was obviously trying to start.

But he wasn't in a good mood.

"Not my fault you can't handle your horse," he said.

"They're both my horses," Cade spat. "Remember? But maybe one day, if your dad works hard enough and does what he's told, my dad will give him a raise. You can save your pennies and buy your own horse. Not one as nice as Joker, of course. Not everyone can afford a good horse."

"You really are a jerk, you know that?" Jesse said. "All because you're jealous of Beau the rodeo star."

Cade pushed Jesse to the ground. Jesse rose halfway and lunged for Cade's legs, knocking him backward and off his feet. Cade landed with a loud *ommpf.*

Off in the distance, a horse screamed. The boys froze. Cade pushed Jesse off him and scrambled to his feet.

"It's the mustang."

CHAPTER 28

THEY RODE INTO A SMALL CLEARING TO A SIGHT THAT STOPPED them dead in their tracks. At first, Jesse thought he was looking at spider webs hanging from the branches of almost every tree; but as he rode toward the center of the clearing he could see the bits of string, yarn, beads, and feathers that adorned the webs.

"What the heck?" Cade said, pushing up out of his saddle to look up and around at the trees.

Jesse recognized Aaron's dreamcatchers. There must be hundreds of them, way more than he had seen in Aaron's bedroom.

Aaron sat on a fallen tree limb, his head in his hands, trembling in the cold rain. Jesse slid off Joker. He grabbed the blanket strapped to his saddlebag, shook it out of its plastic bag, and wrapped it around the other boy.

"Hey, Aaron," he said softly. "Are you okay?"

Aaron looked up, but he didn't answer. His face was streaked with dirt and tears.

"What are you doing, Aaron?"

"Waiting for Reuben."

"Aaron, Reuben's not coming back."

"You're wrong, Jesse. It happened just like I said it would. Reuben is here. I felt him around me as soon as I hung the dreamcatchers in the trees. They worked, Jesse, they really worked."

Jesse stood and turned to Cade.

"We should break out the sleeping bags. The tent, too, since it's raining. It's getting too late to start back down the mountain. We'll stay here tonight."

Cade made no move to dismount. Annoyance flashed across his face.

"Who made you trail boss?"

Kneeling again in front of Aaron, Jesse made a silent decision to ignore Cade.

"I'm going to get you home, Aaron. I promise."

"I'm not leaving without Reuben," Aaron insisted quietly. "I've done everything right. Everything I was supposed to do. I can't leave the mountain until I see him, Jesse."

"We're not leaving yet," Jesse said.

"Why haven't I seen him, Jesse? I feel him all around me. I know Reuben's here. But he won't come to me."

"We'll talk about it tonight, okay? We'll spend tonight in the tent. It'll be fun—a campout."

"Ooooh, I can't wait," Cade said. "A campout with my two best friends—a member of the Future Stable Boys of America Club and a horse thief."

"Back off, Cade," Jesse told him. "Now's not the time."

"Oh, I think it is," Cade said. "You're in big trouble, Aaron, stealing my father's horse."

"I didn't steal anything," Aaron said. "And I'm not afraid of you up here, Cade. I know these woods. I know this mountain. This is Shoshone land…my land. It's a magical place. I've been coming here with Reuben my whole life."

Cade looked around.

"Where's the mustang? Where's my father's horse?"

"He's not here," Aaron said, "and he's not your father's horse. I turned him loose to find Reuben. He's the final Dreamcatcher, the most important one. He's bringing Reuben back to me."

126

"Well, why hasn't he, then?" Cade asked. "You've been here a couple of days. Plenty of time for the magic mustang to find your dead brother's spirit and bring him back alive to you—after it's traveled through the magic dreamcatchers made out of yarn, construction paper, and school glue, of course."

Jesse glared at him.

"You don't have to answer his stupid questions," he told Aaron.

"Jesse's right, Aaron. Don't waste your breath. We can all see that Reuben's not here."

"He's coming!" Aaron insisted. "Wait with me. I know he's coming for me."

Cade gathered Bandit's reins and tugged the horse's head to the left. He stood up in his stirrups, grabbed the nearest dreamcatcher, and pulled it down from the tree. He crumpled it in his fist and shook it at Aaron.

"You know why you haven't seen Reuben? It's because this isn't magic, Aaron. It's crap—just string and yarn and feathers and beads. It's not some magic filter for Reuben's spirit. And it's falling apart in the rain!"

"You don't know anything," Aaron insisted. "Reuben is alive. He's here in these woods."

Cade threw the crumpled dreamcatcher at Aaron.

"You're pathetic. Do you know how stupid that sounds? Your brother's *dead*. String and beads aren't going to bring him back to you. That horse is just some random mustang my mom found in a BLM pen. That's it, Aaron. That's all he is—not magic, not special, not some huge, hairy dreamcatcher. Now, take me to my father's horse. You hear me?"

"He's coming back. He's bringing Reuben. We don't have to search for him." Aaron was openly weeping now; big, glistening tears slid slowly down his face.

Cade clicked his tongue in disgust. He swung Bandit around again and began snatching the dreamcatchers out of the trees and throwing them to the ground.

CHAPTER 28

AARON JUMPED UP.

"What are you doing? Stop it! You'll ruin everything!"

"Tell me where the horse is, Aaron," Cade demanded. "Tell me, and I'll leave your stupid dreamcatchers alone. But I swear I'll rip them all apart if you don't tell me where my father's horse is. I'm taking that horse back down this mountain to my father."

"Stop it, Cade!" Jesse yelled. "We came up here to find *Aaron*, remember? We've got him now. We're going home. Forget the mustang; he's not here."

"This isn't any of your business!" Cade shot back.

"You made it my business when you threatened Aaron," Jesse said. "You ruin another dreamcatcher, I'll pull you right off Bandit."

"How about this, then?" Cade held up a handful of the dreamcatchers he had snatched out of a tree. He leaned out of his saddle, over the edge of a steep ravine. "That's about a fourteen-foot drop, Aaron. Tell me which direction to ride to find the mustang, or I'll drop every one of these."

"You give those back!" Aaron screamed as he rushed across the clearing.

He jumped, grabbing for Cade's arm, but he only made it as high as the saddle pommel. He fell into Bandit and smacked him square on the side of his head. Bandit whinnied in protest. He threw his head up and jigged sideways, knocking Aaron to the edge of the ravine.

Jesse stood only a few feet away, but it might as well have been a mile. Aaron teetered on the soft, wet soil, windmilling his arms in an attempt to keep his balance. By the time Jesse reached him, the small boy was already losing the battle, already falling backward.

Jesse lunged, arms outstretched, in a last-ditch attempt to reach him, but he was too late. Aaron tumbled over the edge of the ravine and plummeted to the bottom, landing with a loud thud.

Fully spooked, Bandit reared and dumped Cade off his back. He bucked once and took off.

Cade groaned as he sat up, still holding a handful of Aaron's dreamcatchers. He scrambled on his hands and knees to the ravine.

"Aaron! Oh, God! Aaron!" He lay with head and shoulders hanging out over the edge, trying to find the other boy in the darkness below. "There he is. I see him!"

Aaron lay on his back, arms and legs in a jumble and his eyes closed. He looked like a marionette that had been carelessly dropped onto the floor.

"He's not moving," Jesse said. "He's not moving at all."

"It was an accident." Cade gestured wildly. "He scared Bandit. It just…it just happened."

The rain chose that moment to become a downpour. Jesse looked skyward as thunder rumbled over the mountain.

"We've got to get him out of there," he said. "If it keeps raining, and the ravine fills up, he'll drown."

Cade swiped at the rain falling in his eyes.

"Look, Jesse, you know I'd never hurt Aaron, right? I just wanted him to tell me where the mustang is."

"It doesn't matter now," Jesse said. "Where's Bandit? We need the rope tied to your saddle. You're going to have to lower me down there."

Both boys took off running. The rain beat down hard on their backs as they rushed to find the horse. Jesse crossed the clearing, heading for a clump of trees and brush. The storm's rage had turned the sky black, but he could just about make out the form of something moving in the brush.

"Over here," he called to Cade.

A flash of lightning illuminated a horse.

It wasn't Bandit.

"You!"

Cade skidded to a muddy stop next to Jesse. Dreamcatcher stood about thirty feet away. Cade looked back over his shoulder toward the ravine. He then turned and took a tentative step toward the mustang.

"What are you doing?" Jesse yelled. How could Cade even think about catching the mustang when Aaron was lying at the bottom of the ravine?

Cade froze as the mustang danced sideways, ready to bolt.

"Go find Bandit, Jesse. Go get the rope."

"You're coming with me. We're getting Aaron out of the ravine!" Jesse ran at the mustang and waved his arms wildly in the air. "Go on, get out here!" he yelled.

The mustang snorted, wheeled, and took off into the darkness of the trees.

Cade rushed at Jesse, who clenched his fists in anticipation.

"What did you do?" he screamed.

"Aaron comes first!" Jesse said.

The thud of approaching hooves came out of the woods.

"He's back!" Cade said. "Stay out of my way, Jesse. I'm getting that horse!"

CHAPTER 29

THE BOYS WHIRLED AROUND JUST AS ANOTHER FLASH OF lightning lit the sky. The mustang snorted, reared, and came straight at them. Cade jumped backward, tripping over his own feet and falling into Jesse. Both boys slipped on the rain-soaked ground and fell.

"Get off me!" Jesse yelled.

They scrambled to their feet.

"Where did he go?" Cade was wide-eyed. "I want that horse!"

"There's Bandit," Jesse yelled over the thunder. He grabbed Bandit's bridle to calm him then undid the lariat that was fastened to the saddle. "The water level in the ravine's rising fast." He straightened the end of the rope, looped it around his waist, and tied a knot. "The mustang won't go far. He doesn't want to leave Aaron. You can get him later. Right now, you have got to help me with Aaron! Okay?"

Cade stood silent, his wet clothes plastered to his body, his blond hair streaming with the rain.

"Do you even have to think about this?" Jesse screamed.

Cade closed his eyes and shook his head.

"No. Of course I'll help Aaron."

Jesse gave the rope a couple tugs to tighten it then threw the other end to Cade.

"Tie that end of the rope to the pommel. Walk backward to take up the slack in the rope." He peered over the edge of the ravine. It was getting difficult to see the bottom. "I'm coming," he called down to Aaron. "Everything's gonna be okay."

He took a deep breath, turned so his back was to the ravine, and grabbed the rope with both hands. He nodded to Cade and stepped back until the heels of his boots were hanging over the edge. Cade backed the quarterhorse up. With the rope taut and secure, Jesse tightened his grip, leaned back, and began to walk down the side of the cliff.

Cade and Bandit disappeared from his view. The wall of rock was only a few feet from his face. An angry wind whistled through the branches of the surrounding trees, and they began to bend and sway. Rustling leaves swirled skyward. A sudden thunderclap cracked the sky with a bang that made him flinch. A flash of lightning lit the sky.

Up above, Cade screamed. The rope went slack. Jesse's feet flew from under him, and he spiraled downward in free-fall. Seconds later, he stopped with a sudden, jarring jolt as the rope caught again. He now swayed and dangled ten feet in the air.

Cade screamed again. The sound of it hit Jesse like a shockwave.

"Cade!" He could hear the panic in his own voice. "Cade! What's happening?"

Silence. Stillness. The only sound was the pounding of the rain on the side of the ravine. Down below, Aaron moaned.

Jesse began kicking, trying to get a swinging motion started. He gradually built up momentum and came in fast and hard, clawing at the side of the ravine. His fingers raked through the soft, wet soil, and he spun off the side of the mountain. He swung again, built up more momentum, but this time, he grabbed onto a tree branch jutting from the ravine wall and held on tight.

Suddenly, the rope pulled tight, jerking him upward. Just as fast, the rope went slack again, and he started to fall. He grabbed at the tree branch and hugged it close to his body.

"Who's up there?" he called. "What do you want?"

The rope started to quiver, and then it pulled taut. Something above was once again taking up the slack. Fear cut through him as the rope tightened painfully around his waist.

He planted his feet against the side of the ravine, took one hand off the tree branch, and frantically tore the rope from around his waist. It flew upward and disappeared over the edge. His heart thumped wildly. He closed his eyes and took a few deep breaths.

Calm down, he told himself. *Gotta calm down for Aaron's sake.*

He looked down and saw water rushing into the ravine. Another flash of lightning showed him Aaron. Water was pooling around the boy.

Jesse dug his hands into the wet soil. He made a careful descent, grabbing every tree branch on the way down. Within ten minutes, his feet touched the bottom.

He rushed to Aaron. He'd learned a long time ago not to move anyone who was badly injured, but he also realized that, this far from home and with the flash flood rising, he really had no choice.

Aaron lay on his back. His eyes fluttered, and he grimaced.

"Hurts," he whispered before closing his eyes again.

Jesse could see a large purple bump on his head, and blood flowed out of his nose and ears. He knelt and ran his hands over Aaron's arms, legs, and chest then breathed a sigh of relief. He was sure Aaron hadn't broken any bones.

He stood and took a close look at the ravine. There were only two ways out: climb straight up the wall he had just come down, or climb up the steep slope on the opposite side.

Climbing straight up the way he'd come, while carrying Aaron, would be impossible. The slope was just as wet, muddy, and slippery, and it would put him on the opposite side of the ravine from Cade and the horses; but it was his only choice.

Jesse shivered. Night was coming, and if Cade didn't appear soon, he and Aaron would be spending the night in the cold and the dark. He looked up, willing the rain to stop. In the back of his mind was also the knowledge that he didn't have a lot of time to get Aaron out of the ravine. If the flood didn't do Aaron in, his injuries might.

He wiped his face with his shirttail, a useless gesture in the pouring rain. A feeling of pure helplessness washed over him. He was determined to fight it off, but as the darkness came, so did the fear.

"Down here! Down here!" he called out. "Cade? Don't leave us! Please don't leave us!"

CHAPTER 30

THE LEVEL OF COLD FLOODWATER ROSE STEADILY OVER THE next hour.

"Cade!" Jesse waited for an answer. And waited. It was dark now, and colder. He picked up a broken tree branch and hurled it at the top of the ravine. "Cade!" he screamed at the top of his lungs. "Cade! Are you all right?"

He took a step backward, splashing in the water that now covered his boots to the ankles. He bent over, put his hands on his knees, and took a few deep breaths. Getting angry wouldn't help. Anger was a distraction.

I need a plan, he thought. *I can't just sit here. If Aaron and I stay at the bottom of the ravine and wait for Cade to help, the water will soon be over our heads.*

He gently grabbed Aaron under the arms and began pulling him up the steep opposite slope. It was hard work; although Aaron was small, he was dead weight right now. The steady rain had turned the hill into a mudslide, preventing Jesse from gaining a firm foothold. He not only had to pull Aaron up the incline but he also had to hold him there so he wouldn't slide back into the bottom of the ravine.

As the night wore on, and the rain continued, Jesse's strength began to fade. He fought hard not to give in to sleep. He was soon shivering, his arms trembling with the effort of keeping Aaron out of the cold rainwater.

When dawn arrived, Jesse lay stretched out on his belly. From the waist up, he was covered in cold mud. From the waist down, he was under the flood that now filled the bottom of the ravine. Aaron lay just above him, halfway up the slope. He was also covered in mud, but at least he was out of the water.

"Aaron?" Jesse croaked. "Are you okay? Please talk to me." When he didn't get an answer, he reached out and gave the boy a gentle shake. He tried bending his knees and moving up next to him, but his legs were numb.

He rested his head on a forearm. It would be so easy to give up right now and right here. He closed his eyes and began to drift away.

He no longer felt the cold mud. No longer felt his wet, stiff clothes. A thousand jumbled images swam before Jesse's eyes—his mom and dad, the mustang, the bear in the stream, the stranger in the gorge, Aaron's dreamcatchers, Aaron…Aaron…Aaron…

Jesse jerked his head up.

"No!" he said out loud. "No! We're getting out of here."

He looked around. The storm clouds had moved on during the night, and thin rays of sunshine were just now beginning to peek through the pine trees. The woods were hushed, quiet. A small doe stared down at him from the top of the hill, lazily chewing a mouthful of grass.

The doe threw her head to the right; something had caught her attention. She stood alert, her ears swiveling. Her white flag of a tail flicked, and she bounded away to the safety of a nearby thicket.

Jesse got up on his knees, groaning as his muscles complained. He crawled up the slope to Aaron's side. Aaron's face was deathly pale, making the purple bruise on his forehead even more noticeable. Jesse stood carefully to test the strength of his legs. He wobbled, lost his balance, fell, and tumbled to the bottom of the ravine, splashing into a pool of cold water.

He came up sputtering and struggled out of the water. He crawled back up to Aaron, ignoring the shakiness in his arms and legs and the pain that sliced through his chest every time he took a breath.

It took him almost an hour, but Jesse managed to drag Aaron up the side of the ravine. He heaved him up onto level ground and collapsed next to him, his breath coming in great ragged gasps. He rolled onto his back, too exhausted to do anything but watch the sun cross the sky and start to sink.

Aaron opened his eyes just as daylight was fading.

"Jesse?" he said weakly. "Where's Cade? Where are the horses?"

"Cade's gone. It's just us."

Aaron squeezed his eyes shut and grimaced. His fists clenched, his body shook, and tears dribbled from the corners of his eyes.

"Hurts bad," he whispered. When the spasm passed, he wiped his eyes and looked at Jesse. "Over there, Jesse. Look."

Jesse sat up.

"You see Cade? Where is he?"

"No." Aaron pointed to the woods. "Over there."

The mustang stood where the doe had been a few hours earlier. He took a few steps toward the boys then stopped and shook his head. Jesse's heart was racing, but he stayed completely still.

This is our chance to get down the mountain.

The mustang trotted over, dropped his nose to Aaron, and took a long sniff. He nickered long and low, and then he nudged the boy.

"Hey, boy," Aaron's voice was barely a whisper now. He closed his eyes.

Jesse pushed up onto his hands and knees. He stood and took a few faltering steps toward the mustang. Dreamcatcher shook his head and looked back at the woods, but he stood still.

"Good boy." Jesse reached out to stroke the mustang's neck. "We're going to take Aaron home."

He wrapped his arms around the mustang's neck and clung for a moment, his legs trembling uncontrollably. Wavy lines danced across his vision, and a sudden feeling of lightheadedness threatened to send him crashing down on top of Aaron. He gritted his teeth and waited it out before bending down and grabbing Aaron under his arms.

He heaved with all his might, trying to lift the other boy onto the mustang's back, but his legs gave out. He crumpled to the ground, taking Aaron with him. Aaron cried out in pain.

"I'm sorry, Aaron. So sorry."

Jesse inhaled deeply and tried again. This time, he felt someone behind him, helping push Aaron up onto Dreamcatcher's back. He turned, expecting to see Cade.

No one was there.

I'm losing it, he thought.

"Hold on to him, Aaron. Grab his mane."

He steadied Aaron as he led Dreamcatcher to a large rock he could use as a mounting block. Once seated behind Aaron, he grabbed the boy by the waist and hugged him tight to his chest.

He knew Savage Ranch lay to the west. He had no reins, but he was able to use his left leg to get the mustang to turn. Dreamcatcher started to walk, slowly at first, but then with determination, picking his way through the trees and scrub, following the setting sun.

CHAPTER 31

AT SOME POINT DURING THE RIDE DOWN THE MOUNTAIN, Aaron stopped talking. Jesse hardly noticed; fatigue and the effects of spending the previous night lying in a pool of cold rainwater caught up with him, and he could no longer force his eyes to remain open. His arms and legs continued to ache, and his chest burned with each breath. He drifted between sleep and wakefulness, his head on his chest, nodding in rhythm with Dreamcatcher's gait.

He didn't know how long he was on the mustang's back or even how they made it back to Savage Ranch. When he rode onto the ranch the next morning and heard the surprised voices of Ellie, Beau, and some of the ranch hands, he was sure he was dreaming. Nothing seemed real. Not the fact that Dreamcatcher had found his way back. Not that one moment he and Aaron were miles away, and the next they were home.

Especially not that, whenever he had been on the brink of losing his balance and falling off the mustang, he'd felt a strong pair of arms wrap around his waist and keep him upright.

Cade was there, too.

That can't be right, Jesse thought. *Cade's lost in the woods with Joker and Bandit.*

But then why were the quarterhorses standing unsaddled in a corral, swishing flies away with great sweeps of their tails?

Jesse saw his father running toward him, saw Big Bob beside him pulling a cell phone from his pocket and punching numbers on its keypad. Beau reached for Aaron as Jesse fell into his father's arms.

Cade walked up to Dreamcatcher and slipped a halter over the mustang's head. He then clipped a lead rope to the halter. His face was blank as he led the mustang over to Big Bob and handed him the end of the rope.

Jesse struggled in his father's arms. He wanted to yell at Cade, but the words wouldn't come. He watched Ellie put her arms around Cade and hug him. Cade looked down and covered his face with his hands. Mother and son left the stables for the big house, disappearing behind the front door.

Jesse blinked hard in an effort to keep his eyes open, but it was a losing battle. He wanted to accuse Cade of caring more about the mustang than about Aaron, and he wanted everyone to hear.

You left us! You left us up on the mountain!

He heard the words so clearly in his own head. Why were his father, Big Bob, and Beau just standing there? Why was Dreamcatcher, now bucking, rearing, and screaming, being forcefully led away as Aaron was loaded into an ambulance?

Jesse blinked once more then surrendered to the darkness.

CHAPTER 32

JESSE'S EYELIDS FELT AS IF SOMEONE HAD HUNG TINY WEIGHTS on them. Waking up in the hospital was like sailing out of a thick fog. He knew he was in a hospital bed, but he couldn't remember how he'd gotten here or how long it had been.

He slowly became aware of a conversation going on above him. He heard women's voices, one that he recognized. He struggled to lift his head off the pillow for a better look, but he didn't have the strength.

The woman noticed his movement. She leaned in closer, coming into focus.

It was his mom.

"Hi," she said.

Jesse licked his lips and tried to speak. His mouth was dry, and his tongue felt like sandpaper.

"Hi," he finally croaked.

The other woman, a nurse, checked his IV line and left the room.

"I'm happy to see you awake, Jesse," she called on her way out. "I'm going to call your doctor."

Kate Alvarez took hold of Jesse's hand.

"Your dad called me." Her eyes welled with tears. "I was so worried."

"We messed up bad. Aaron got hurt."

"Aaron might have died if you hadn't gotten him out of those woods. Nobody knew where he was."

"Is he here at the hospital?"

Kate nodded.

"He's in the ICU. He's been unconscious since you brought him in."

Tears gathered in the corners of Jesse's eyes. He had thought about the moment he would see his mom again for years. It didn't seem real she was now standing in front of him.

"We have a home now, Mom. Did you know that? Did you know that Dad's a foreman?"

Kate nodded again.

"I'm proud of him. He works so hard; he deserves that kind of job."

"Will you come visit us, Mom? When I get out of here, you could come see our home."

"Let's concentrate on getting you well before we talk about that, Jesse. I know you don't understand, but—"

"No, I don't understand," he interrupted. "I don't understand why you left. I don't understand why you haven't come back. I don't understand how you can say you love me when you don't want to see me."

"I see you, Jesse. Every day of my life, I see you."

The tears that had gathered in the corners of Jesse's eyes spilled down the sides of his face and onto his pillow.

"I don't care what happened. You're my mom. You're perfect no matter what. Why can't you understand that?"

There was a knock at the door; Big Bob poked his head into the room.

146

"Just stopped by to see how Jesse's doing. I can come back if this is a bad time."

"It's fine, Mr. Savage. I've got to get going anyway."

"No, Mom, don't go. You just got here."

"Jesse, I've been here for three days."

"You've been out of it, buddy," Big Bob said. "But Mrs. Alvarez, please don't leave on account of me."

"I'd like to have one more minute alone with Jesse, please."

"Of course." Big Bob stepped out of the room, closing the door behind him.

Kate pulled a chair close to Jesse's bed.

"First of all, I'm not going far. I'm living in Lander with my aunt Gwen. Secondly, I've got something for you." She reached into her pocket and pulled out a cell phone. "This is brand new. It has only one number in the contacts—mine."

She held out the phone to him. He reached up slowly and took it.

"Does Dad know?"

"Of course. From now on, you don't have to go to his office to talk to me. Call me, Jesse—for any reason. If you just want to talk, if you're having a problem at school, if you're planning a rescue mission up in the mountains with Cade Savage…"

Jesse couldn't help but smile.

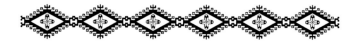

CHAPTER 33

JESSE WAS DISCHARGED FROM THE HOSPITAL A FEW DAYS LATER. He'd been treated for dehydration and pneumonia and still felt a little wobbly on his feet. The doctor insisted he spend some time recuperating at home, so Jesse used the time to make up his missed schoolwork.

He had only recently taken his first walk around the ranch since riding up into the mountains. The mustang was gone, his corral empty. And Aaron was still in the hospital. Still in the intensive care unit.

He carried the cell phone with him wherever he went. He pulled it out of his pocket a lot, turning it over-and-over in his hand, enjoying the smoothness of it. His mom had called him just to make sure he was feeling better. He had even visited with her at Aunt Gwen's, but he was thrilled when she agreed to a visit at his house.

He'd planned on surprising both his parents by fixing dinner. They did look surprised when they walked through the front door and saw the table set and the stove littered with pots and pans, but it wasn't a "good surprised," he saw.

Neither Mark nor Kate smiled as they sat down. They talked, but it wasn't the family dinner he'd hoped for.

Maybe it was the food, he thought. *Yeah, that's it. I'll fix something better next time.*

Cade hadn't been around the stables much, which suited Jesse just fine. He imagined Cade was proud of having brought the mustang back, so when he rounded the corner of an equipment shed and almost tripped over him, he was shocked. Cade looked terrible; he had dark circles under his eyes, and he was pale and shaky.

Cade braced himself against the shed wall, a leg bent up under his body.

"I need to talk to you, Jesse."

Jesse continued past him.

"I've got nothing to say to you."

"Jesse…please."

Jesse sighed and stopped. He turned to face Cade.

"What?"

Cade closed his eyes and leaned his head back against the shed wall. He swallowed hard.

"That night…on the mountain. He came out of the darkness."

"Who?"

"The stranger we saw at the gorge. At least I thought he was a stranger until I got a good look at him. I took Bandit and Joker, and I know I left you and Aaron, but I was so scared.

"And now I *keep* seeing him. No matter where I am—he's there. When I wake up in the morning. When I close my eyes at night. He's in my dreams. He won't leave me alone."

"Who?"

"Reuben Little Elk."

"Not funny. " Jesse began to walk away.

"You were right," Cade called. "Someone was following us up on the mountain. It was Reuben. I know that now. He was at the gorge. He relit the fire. I know it was him you saw at the gates your first day at the ranch."

Jesse turned and said, "Do you hear how crazy that sounds?"

"I didn't tell you this before, but that red-beaded headband? Aaron made a headband like that for Reuben. He wore it all the time. He talked for months in school about the stupid thing."

"Like you said before, Cade, lots of Indian men around have long hair and wear beaded headbands."

"Someone helped you get Aaron down the mountain. That's what you said. My dad told me. Someone was holding you from behind as you rode the mustang. Are you saying now it was your imagination? It didn't really happen?"

Jesse was silent for a moment.

"No, I'm not saying it didn't happen."

"Who was is it, Jesse?" Cade was almost shouting. "Who did you see?"

"No one," Jesse said. His own voice was rising now. "I didn't see anyone. I don't know what happened. All I know is that, somehow, Aaron and I got down the mountain."

"It's Aaron who should be seeing him, not me, and not you," Cade said. "It's Aaron who did crazy stuff with those dreamcatchers. Something got messed up. We've got to make it right."

"We? *We?*" Jesse walked over and stood in front of him. "If you hadn't acted like such an idiot when we found Aaron, the horse wouldn't be gone, and Aaron wouldn't be in the hospital."

Cade kicked off of the wall and stood up straight.

"I know where he is—the mustang. We can get him. It was a mistake for you to bring him back."

"I *didn't* bring him back," Jesse said. "*He* brought *me* back—saved me, saved Aaron after you left us up on the mountain. Aaron and I could have died if Dreamcatcher hadn't found us at the ravine. We were lucky."

"It wasn't luck, it was Reuben. You saw his headband. That proves it."

Jesse turned to leave, but Cade grabbed his sleeve. He pulled a photograph from his back pocket and pushed it into Jesse's hand.

"Look at this. It's Beau and Reuben Little Elk at a party my dad had for the trainers and ranch hands a few years ago. Same pattern on the headband, right? Tell me that's not the man you saw at the gates and at the gorge."

It does look like the same man, Jesse thought as he took a long look at Reuben. He thrust the picture back at Cade.

"Doesn't make sense. Reuben Little Elk is dead."

"I know what I'm seeing, and I'm not crazy," Cade said. "The mustang is the key; I know he is. The key to Aaron getting better, and the key to Reuben leaving. I've thought about this a lot. We've got to take the mustang back up to the mountain. We've got to free him."

CHAPTER 34

"JUST HOW ARE WE GOING TO DO THAT, CADE?" JESSE ASKED.
"I know. We could do it ourselves. Let's sneak out in the middle of the night, take the horses, and go up into the mountains. Oh, wait, we tried that." He smacked his head. "Didn't work out so well."

"I wasn't talking about us going by ourselves."

"Who, then? Your dad? My dad? Get real. They're not going to believe Reuben's stalking you."

"No, not them."

The realization of what Cade was suggesting finally hit Jesse.

"No way," he said.

"Call her, Jesse. It's the only way we'll be able to help Aaron."

"Help *Aaron*? You just want to help yourself. You feel so guilty about what you did you think you're seeing his dead brother. What was it you called him when we were up on the mountain? When he was waiting for Reuben? Oh, yeah, you called him pathetic."

"I know it doesn't make sense, Jesse, but we've got to try. You're Aaron's friend. I know you'd do whatever it takes to get him better. Well, your mom is the only one who can help us."

"You don't know anything about my mom!" Jesse was angry now. "What can she do? Your father's not going to let us take the horse."

"The horse isn't at the ranch. He's at the auction pens. You know what that means, don't you, Jesse? We both know what that means. "

"Your father wouldn't send a horse to auction."

"My father cares for his horses, but he's also a businessman. You don't know what that horse has been like since he's been back."

"He wouldn't *be* back if it wasn't for you," Jesse said.

Cade bit his bottom lip and nodded.

"Right," he admitted. "I put that lead rope in my father's hands, and at the time, I felt good about it. My dad was proud of me. You were right about me…and Beau. He's always been good at everything, no matter what it was. Riding. School. The rodeo. Especially the rodeo. He could have been famous.

"But he gave it up, turned his back on all of it—the fame, the money—for my dad. I'd have done it too. I'd…" Cade's voice broke. He turned his back to Jesse and wiped his eyes quickly with his shirt cuff. Then he cleared his throat. "I'd do anything for my dad. But I have nothing to give him. Nothing at all." He cleared his throat again. "My dad will never be as proud of me as he is of Beau."

Jesse's desire to keep yelling at Cade disappeared. You didn't kick someone when he was down, no matter how much you disliked him.

"Anyway." Cade turned to face him. "The mustang went completely nuts. He charged at anyone who tried to get close to him. My dad won't keep a dangerous horse. He never has."

"I guess that's it, then," Jesse said. "There's not much we can do."

"There's *one* thing, Jesse. Call her." Cade was pleading now, but Jesse didn't take any pleasure from it. "She hasn't seen you in forever, right? I bet she'd say yes to you because she feels so…you know…guilty."

Jesse could only shake his head. He began to hurry away from Cade.

"The meat man's going to get him!" Cade called after him. "Kill buyers stake out that auction."

Jesse stopped. That was bad news. There *was* only one destination for a horse with a past at the auction. *Would* his mom help them? And if she did, would it be out of guilt? What if she turned him down?

The thought of that happening made Jesse very sad. He started walking again. He didn't look back to see if Cade was still there. He met his dad back at the house, and they drove to visit Aaron in the hospital.

CHAPTER 35

THE NURSE WAVED JESSE INTO THE ICU WHILE HIS DAD TOOK a seat in the waiting room. The rules said only Aaron's family was allowed to visit, but he had gotten special permission in hopes his being there might help.

"Come on in. There's not much change, I'm afraid."

Jesse gazed down at Aaron.

"Has he woken up at all?"

"No." The nurse rubbed Jesse's arm. "I'm so sorry. He's hanging in there. Had a rough time last night, though."

"There has to be something else, something you haven't tried."

"We've done everything that needs to be done for Aaron. He should be better. It's up to him now. I don't know what he's waiting for."

Jesse watched as she checked Aaron's tubes and turned some dials on the machine that was hooked up to his IV.

"What did you mean when you said Aaron had a rough night?" Jesse asked.

"Poor little thing thrashes and cries out, like he's having a bad dream."

"Aaron's having bad dreams again?" Jesse said.

The nurse nodded.

"Really bad dreams. Happens almost every night." She straightened Aaron's blanket and left the room.

Jesse pulled the cell phone out of his pocket and held it tightly in his hand. Was Aaron dreaming about Reuben again? Was it the dream where he found Reuben on the ground and…?

He shook his head; he couldn't bear to think about it.

I'm going to take a chance. If she says no, I'll deal with it. This is about Aaron, not me.

He flipped the phone open and dialed. Kate Alvarez answered almost immediately.

"Jesse?"

He took a deep breath.

"Mom," he said. "I need your help. Aaron needs your help."

CHAPTER 36

*"WHERE IS SHE? YOU SAID SHE'D BE HERE." CADE PACED REST-*lessly in front of the largest stable.

"She will be," Jesse said. "Relax. You're starting to make me nervous."

"Maybe she changed her mind. Maybe your dad talked her out of coming. I still can't believe she called my dad."

"She would never have agreed to help us if it meant going behind our dads' backs."

"Did you tell her about Reuben?" Cade asked.

"No. I didn't know how to explain that part. I don't think anyone who wasn't up there on the mountain with us could understand."

Twenty minutes later, a red Ford F-150 pickup pulling a slant-load gooseneck horse trailer turned into the parking lot. Kate climbed out of the driver's side and walked toward the boys. She was wearing a navy blue T-shirt, jeans, and boots. Her honey-blonde hair was pulled into a ponytail. Jesse's breath caught in his throat at the sight of her.

He gave the truck and trailer an admiring glance.

"Nice rig."

"Borrowed the trailer from my aunt; the truck's mine."

"And you're really okay with this, Mom?"

"I know how special this horse is to Aaron, and I'm going to do what I can to get him out of that awful place. I'd do just about anything to save a horse from slaughter. But Mr. Savage warned me the horse has been unpredictable lately. I won't put either of you boys in a dangerous situation. I want you both to understand that from the get-go. Okay?"

"Okay, Mom."

"Yes, Mrs. Alvarez."

The drive to the New Market horse auction took forty-five minutes. It was late morning by the time they arrived, and the auction grounds and parking lots were crowded. Buyers, sellers, and those who came merely to gawk milled around as Kate navigated through a sea of pickup trucks and horse trailers until she found a parking space.

"All right," she said, "why don't we start by looking inside the big building just to make sure he's not going up for auction soon."

"We could split up and cover more ground," Cade suggested. "I'll look outside in the pens and small corrals next to the auction house."

"Okay," Kate agreed, "but you boys stick together. Call me if you see him."

For the next twenty minutes, the boys wandered among the pens.

"Are you sure your father sent him to this auction?" Jesse asked. "I've seen paints and pintos and none of them are Dreamcatcher."

"I know he's here," Cade said. "There's your mom. Maybe she spotted him."

"Any luck?" Jesse called.

"No," Kate said. "Nothing inside looks remotely close to a paint mustang." She approached a cowboy throwing

160

hay into one of the pens. "Will any more horses be coming in today?"

"No, but there's some corrals around the back of the auction house," the cowboy said. He was an older man, very thin, with gnarled hands and a green wild-rag tied around his neck. "Don't get too many people back there; horses in those pens were already bought by Mike Hughes. They won't be going into the auction."

Jesse watched the color drain from Cade's face.

"Is that bad?" Jesse asked.

"He's a kill buyer, a meat man. He buys horses here and then sends them to slaughter. He's paid per pound."

"I'm driving the rest of this hay around there now," the old cowboy said. "Feel free to follow me."

Kate found the kill buyer's corrals. There were ten in all, five on either side of a center dirt pathway. She parked the truck in front of the path, pulling the rig across two parking spaces so the trailer faced the corrals. They climbed out of the truck and walked down the center, scanning the corrals. A few horses were in the front pens, but not one was a paint mustang.

Cade ran to the back pens, the ones farthest from the parking lot.

"There he is!"

Dreamcatcher stood alone in a muddy corral.

"Word around here is that one's dangerous," the old cowboy, who had ridden over with them, said. "Took a hunk out of Mike Hughes's arm!" He laughed. "Doesn't make him dangerous, in my estimation. Makes him a good judge of character."

"We have to find Mike Hughes," Kate said. "Cade, can you point him out to me?"

"You don't have to look for him, ma'am," the cowboy said, pointing over her shoulder. "He's right over there in the parking lot talking to his driver."

Kate crossed her fingers for good luck.

"Okay, guys, think positive. I'll be right back."

Jesse propped his foot up on a fence rail and watched as she went over to Mike Hughes. He had expected a kill buyer to look as evil as the job he did, but Hughes looked, well, ordinary. He wasn't short or tall, fat or thin. He had sandy brown hair and a face you wouldn't remember at the end of the day.

He and Cade watched Hughes smile politely and reach out to shake Kate's hand. He leaned forward and appeared to listen intently to her. Then he shook his head and walked away.

She came back, hands pushed deep into her pockets, a dejected look on her face.

"No go," she said. "He said he'll get more money from the slaughterhouse in Mexico than I have to offer."

"I've got some money, too, Mom," Jesse reached into his pocket. "I've saved everything Mr. Savage paid me for working around the ranch."

"It's still not enough," Kate said. They stood silent for a minute. "I'm going to call my aunt, see if she can help."

"We don't have a lot of time," Cade said. "Hughes is about to cram all the horses he bought into a trailer. That driver he was talking to just climbed into the cab. He's only waiting for the stock to be loaded."

Kate opened the driver's side door of her truck. She climbed in and pulled out the purse she had stowed under the seat.

"I need her work number."

Jesse, his eyes still on his mom, began to inch back from the truck and trailer. Cade noticed.

"What are you doing ?" he asked.

"Just be ready," Jesse said in a low voice.

CHAPTER 37

HE DIDN'T WAIT FOR CADE'S REPLY. HE TURNED AND SPRINTED toward the back corral where Dreamcatcher was biding time until he would be loaded onto a trailer with the rest of the slaughter-bound.

They were horses, he knew, who'd dared to commit the great crime of growing old or turning up lame. Horses who'd spent countless hours carrying child after child around the same arena in lesson after lesson. Horses who'd been faithful friends and companions, and who deserved a peaceful retirement, not abandonment and a cruel death.

He slid between the slats of the fence and crouched low to the ground, hoping Mike Hughes hadn't seen him. Dreamcatcher noticed him immediately and snorted.

"Shhh!" Jesse put a finger to his lips.

There were voices behind him now—men's voices. He turned, poked his head up, and locked eyes with the old cowboy wearing the green wild-rag. The cowboy's eyes widened, his gaze flitting from Jesse to Dreamcatcher and back to Jesse again.

Then Mike Hughes came into view. Jesse ducked, but Hughes went on talking; the kill buyer had not seen him.

He was far too busy yelling at the old cowboy to notice anyone or anything around him.

"For crying out loud, Pete, I've told you before to stop putting so much hay in my pens. Those horses don't need it where they're going. I'm getting charged per bale, and the dang things are eating into my profits."

"They're hungry, Mr. Hughes. And they've got a rough ride ahead of them, the way you pack them in the trailer. Ain't humane, in my opinion."

"You want them broke-down things, Pete? You going to feed them, pay their vet bills?"

"You know I can't, Mr. Hughes. I'm just saying it can't hurt to give them a little comfort, considering what's waiting for them." Pete moved in front of Hughes, completely blocking the kill buyer's view of Jesse. He casually reached behind him and pulled the gate latch up.

"You want to comfort those horses, Pete, you go right ahead. Give them all a big hug while you're at it. But you pay for it," Hughes said.

"Just saying what's on my mind." Pete stretche his left foot to the bottom of the gate and pried it open a few inches.

Still squatting in the pen in front of the mustang, Jesse considered his chances. If he waited too long, Hughes was bound to notice the gate was open.

Praying Dreamcatcher wouldn't spook, Jesse sprang up from the ground and launched himself onto the mustang's back. He grabbed fistfuls of Dreamcatcher's mane and squeezed his legs firmly into the horse's sides.

"Go!" he shouted. He urged Dreamcatcher toward the gate, but the mustang veered to the right and ran to the back of the pen. "No, boy!" He squeezed with his legs again. Dreamcatcher stopped and whinnied loudly.

The commotion stopped Mike Hughes in his tracks. Confusion spread across his face.

"Hey! Hey, kid!" he called. "What the heck you think you're doing? Get down off of my horse!"

"Hear that, boy?" Jesse whispered into Dreamcatcher's ear. "He thinks you're his. But you're not, are you? You belong to Aaron. You should be running free up in the mountains. You stay here with that man…" He nodded toward Hughes. "…and you're gonna wind up on a menu somewhere in France. Let's go, okay, boy?"

Dreamcatcher snorted and half-reared. He took off like a shot, heading straight for the gate. If Jesse had not been holding onto his mane, he would have been left on the ground to eat the mustang's dust.

The old cowboy tried to keep his body between Mike Hughes and the gate, but the younger man simply pushed by him.

"Dang it, Pete, what are you doing? Get out of the way!" Hughes slammed the gate closed and slid the latch back into place. "Ha, got you now, kid!"

"Whoa, boy," Jesse called, pulling on Dreamcatcher's mane, trying to slow him down.

But Dreamcatcher didn't slow, didn't react to Jesse's hands at all; he never even broke his stride as he approached the gate. Jesse felt the horse gather himself, felt Dreamcatcher's determination as he increased his speed.

He flashed back to the race with Cade and Bandit when the mustang had opened his stride and run the way a fierce wind blows. He gritted his teeth and leaned forward in anticipation.

The smug look on Mike Hughes's face was quickly replaced with one of shock as Dreamcatcher continued to run straight at him and the closed gate.

"Don't be stupid, kid!" Hughes shouted. "Don't try it. Pull him up! Pull him up!"

Pete made a grab for Hughes's arm.

"Open the gate, Mr. Hughes! The boy's gonna get hurt!" Hughes shook him off.

"Boy knows what's good for him, he'll pull the dang horse up and stop him."

"The boy ain't the one in charge, Mr. Hughes. Look at that horse! Look at the crazy bugger! He wants out of here! Open the gate. It ain't worth the boy getting hurt."

Hughes made a move toward the gate, but it was too late. Dreamcatcher was bearing down on him. He didn't have the time to open the gate now, even though he wanted to.

Dreamcatcher jumped, soaring over the gate and over Mike Hughes, who dropped to his knees to avoid the hooves that were now directly in line with his head.

Jesse bounced as Dreamcatcher landed, but he stayed on the mustang's back. As Dreamcatcher sped away, Jesse heard Pete whooping and hollering.

"Stop that kid!" Mike Hughes gave chase, waving his arms in the air. "Horse thief! Horse thief! That kid's stealing my horse!"

CHAPTER 38

*DREAMCATCHER GALLOPED AT FULL SPEED ALONG THE CEN-*ter path. Fence posts, horses, buildings flashed by in a blur. Jesse's eyes began to tear as the horse's speed increased.

Auction-goers, drawn by the noise and the sight of a horse galloping through the kill pens, began to appear along the corral fences. They waved their hats and cheered Jesse on.

Up ahead on his left, three men were running across the center of a corral. They scrambled over the fence and jumped into the path in an attempt to block Dreamcatcher's escape.

"Slow down, kid," one of the cowboys shouted, throwing his hands up in the air.

"No way," Jesse shouted back. "Not today. You're not getting this one."

He tugged on Dreamcatcher's mane. The mustang responded by cutting to his right and flying over the closest corral fence. As they galloped through the corral, Jesse pulled the wad of bills out of his pocket and threw it over his head in the direction of the three cowboys.

"Give this to Mike Hughes!" he called as Dreamcatcher jumped the fence again and landed in the parking lot. "I've got chore money coming, too!"

Kate and Cade were standing at the back of the trailer. Jesse was close enough now to see their jaws drop in surprise as he and Dreamcatcher approached, kicking up clouds of dust at a full gallop. The three cowboys and Mike Hughes weren't far behind; Jesse glanced over his shoulder and saw the four men sprinting through the same corral Dreamcatcher had just jumped from.

"Oh, good lord," Kate said. She ran to start the truck.

"The ramp!" Cade called. "We've got to get the ramp down!"

They made a mad scramble to let the trailer ramp down.

Dreamcatcher slowed as he approached the trailer. He flattened his ears and threw a small buck, a clear indication to Jesse that if he allowed the horse to stop and look at the trailer, he'd never get him up the ramp.

I understand, boy, he thought. *Trailers have never taken you anywhere good.*

"You've got to trust me, boy," he said, squeezing the mustang's sides to encourage him up the ramp. "Aaron needs you to go with us."

Dreamcatcher whinnied and bolted up the ramp. Jesse slid off the mustang's back and jumped out of the trailer.

"Cade, hurry, help me!"

They raised the ramp and secured it, then threw themselves into Kate's truck. With tires spinning and gravel flying, they peeled out of the parking lot.

"Go, go, go, Mom!" Jesse shouted.

Kate took a quick look in a side mirror.

"Anybody coming after us?"

Jesse craned his neck out the window and around the trailer. The men had just reached the parking lot. They slowed, jogged a few more feet, then stopped running altogether.

"Nope, looks like they're giving up," he said as Mike Hughes snatched his hat off his head and threw it to the ground in disgust.

Kate left the auction grounds, joining the traffic heading back to Riverton. Safely on the road, they started laughing.

"My heart's still pounding," she said. "I can't believe you, Jesse! Where on earth did you learn to ride like that?"

Jesse flushed with pride. He shrugged.

"It was nothing."

Thirty minutes later, they drove past Savage Ranch, heading for the Wind River Reservation and Mountains, trying to get as close as possible to the canyon where Aaron had let Dreamcatcher go. Kate pulled off the road onto a small dirt path. She parked under the cover of a few tall cedar trees and brought out a map.

"We can't get as close with the truck as you guys did on horseback," she said. "We're going to have to walk him in."

Jesse and Cade let the trailer ramp down. Dreamcatcher was alert, ears pricked forward, eyes bright—but he was also calm. He blew air through his nostrils as Jesse haltered him, attached a lead rope, and backed him out of the trailer.

Jesse nodded at Cade.

"Let's go."

"Wait," Kate said. "I'm coming with you."

"Mom, no."

"I'm not letting you go alone, Jesse."

"I won't be alone, Mom. Cade will be with me."

"You know what I mean, Jesse. After what happened. And you said some strange man followed you."

Jesse walked up and hugged her. Kate's eyes brimmed with sudden tears.

"Nothing's going to happen, Mom," he whispered. "We'll be back in no time. I promise. It was just Cade and me up there the first time. It has to be just Cade and me this time, too." He released her and backed away.

Kate used the palms of her hands to wipe her eyes.

"Okay," she said. "Okay. Go now, before I come to my senses and change my mind."

CHAPTER 39

THE BOYS SET OFF WITH DREAMCATCHER BETWEEN THEM.
Jesse reached up and stroked the mustang's neck, and he
nickered in response.

They walked until the trail gradually faded to wild scrub
and red rock. Jesse handed the mustang's lead rope to Cade
and climbed onto a rock ledge. There was a faint gurgling
in the distance.

"It's the river," he said. "Canyon's just beyond the hill."

"But we were on the other side of the canyon. This
isn't the right place."

Jesse jumped down off of the ledge, raising a small cloud
of red dust under the heels of his boots.

"It took us two days to get over there, Cade. This is as
close as we're going to get just walking in."

Cade clicked his tongue at Dreamcatcher and pulled
lightly on the lead rope to get him going. The mustang
stopped in his tracks and refused to move forward. Cade
grabbed the mustang's halter and tried giving it a tug, but
Dreamcatcher pulled away and whinnied loudly. His in-
sistent call echoed throughout the woods.

Cade, eyes narrowed, scanned the trees. The forest had gone still.

"He's here," he whispered.

He unbuckled the halter. The mustang pulled out of it with a grunt. He wheeled and whinnied again.

"There!" Jesse had caught a flash of buckskin through the trees, a shadowy figure.

"Reuben, stop!" Cade yelled. "We've brought the mustang."

There was a sudden electricity in the air, and the hairs on Jesse's arms and the back of his neck stood up. He took off without a word, crashing through the scrub and pushing through thickets and branches. He caught glimpses of the figure ahead, arms pumping, black hair streaming, weaving through the trees.

Jesse ran until he lost sight of the figure. He stopped and doubled over, breathing hard, and realized he was alone, deep in the woods. Slender rays from the late-afternoon sun slanted sideways through the trees and lit up a small object laying on the forest floor. He knelt and reached for it. It was the red-beaded headband.

The low drumming of hooves sounded behind Jesse. Dreamcatcher broke through the scrub and thundered past, whinnying for Reuben. Cade arrived a minute later, out of breath. He squeezed his sides as he reached Jesse and stood over him.

"He's gone," Cade said. "It's over. I don't feel him anymore. The mustang's free, and so am I."

"It's not over for Aaron, is it. He's still in the hospital," Jesse said. "All you care about is how it affects you."

"That's not true. I—"

Jesse stood and turned away from Cade. He was suddenly bone-tired. The adrenaline he had been running on all day was gone. He pushed the headband into his pants pocket and headed back to Kate's truck.

The drive back to Savage Ranch was quiet. When Kate parked in front of the stables to let Cade out, he leaned toward her.

"Thanks, Mrs. Alvarez." He climbed out of the truck but didn't close the door. "Thanks, Jesse," he added.

"I did it for Aaron."

The saddest of smiles tugged at Cade's lips.

"I know," he said.

CHAPTER 40

KATE PULLED INTO THE FRONT YARD OF JESSE AND MARK'S house. She put the truck in park and leaned back in her seat.

"Do you want to come in?" Jesse asked. "I could get you a glass of iced tea, or something to eat."

"It's been a long day, Jesse. I…"

"He's not here, Mom. He's at work."

Kate turned and looked at him.

"I'm not worried about seeing your father, Jesse."

"Then what is it, Mom? If it's not Dad, it must have been me."

"Don't you ever think that, Jesse. Ever."

"Why not? What am I supposed to think when you won't tell me?" Jesse reached over and turned the ignition off. "I used to lay in bed and wonder what I did or said to make you leave me."

"I didn't leave you, Jesse."

"Oh, yeah? Because that's what it felt like. What it still feels like." He felt both anger and sadness pulsate through him. He had done amazing things today. He had been smart and daring and courageous. At this moment, though, he was just a thirteen-year-old boy struggling to understand why the mother he worshipped had left him.

Kate smiled and reached over to brush a lock of hair from his forehead.

"Your dad and I were so young when we had you. Lord, if I only knew then what I know now."

"Fine," Jesse said. "I get it. You're not going to tell me." He flung open the door, jumped out, slammed it shut, and strode off toward the house.

"Jesse?"

He turned to find her jogging toward him.

"Let's take a walk," she said.

They wandered along the banks of the stream behind the house until they found a place to sit. Kate took her shoes off and stuck her feet into the water.

"Oh, that feels so good," she said. "Nice and cool." She looked over at Jesse and smiled. "You're a good boy with a great heart."

He sat, silent and watching. Waiting.

"I was seventeen years old when I first met your dad," Kate began. A slow smile spread across her face as she remembered. "I was in my senior year of high school, and I was bored, bored, bored. Bored with school. Bored with my friends. Bored with myself."

"But you were so lucky. Your family had horses, and you barrel-raced and competed in shows," Jesse said. "Didn't you like doing that?"

"Sure, I liked it, but I was a daydreamer full of romantic notions about life. I was convinced that nothing good or exciting would happen in the small town where I lived.

"Well, one night—it was a school night, actually—I snuck out to meet my best friend and go to the rodeo."

Jesse was surprised. It was hard enough imagining his parents as teenagers, even harder to imagine them sneaking out of the house or disobeying parents.

"Your dad was there. He was nineteen years old, and and he was soooooo cute."

Jesse squeezed his eyes shut, screwed up his face.

"Mom."

"Well, he was," Kate said. "Serious, too—he seemed to know exactly what he wanted to do with his life."

"Dad knew he wanted to be a ranch hand when he was nineteen?"

She looked at him for a minute before answering.

"Of course not. He dreamed of owning a big ranch and breeding champion horses. He was full of big ideas and plans."

"He never told me any of that," Jesse said.

Kate leaned forward and dipped two fingers into the stream, trailing them along the surface of the water, creating tiny ripples.

"Well, that's because he stopped talking about it a long time ago."

CHAPTER 41

JESSE FELT A SUDDEN LUMP IN HIS THROAT.

"He gave up on his dreams. It was because of me, wasn't it? Because you had me."

Kate pulled her hand out of the stream and shook the water off of her fingers.

"Your dad loves you, Jesse. Just as I do. Having you was the best thing that ever happened to us."

"So, Dad gave up his dream of owning a ranch and you left me because things were great? " Jesse heard the harsh tone in his voice. What was he doing? He had longed to be with his mom like this for years. Why couldn't he stop acting this way?

"I never said things were great." Her tone had turned serious, almost sad, and Jesse briefly wondered, *Do I really want to hear this?*

Kate continued. "Your dad and I got married right after I graduated from high school. He was working as a rodeo laborer. He'd saved almost every penny he earned to put toward his ranch."

"So, why didn't he buy it," Jesse asked.

"I got pregnant with you almost right away. And babies need more than love, Jesse. They need diapers, and food, and clothing, medicine and a clean place to live. The money your dad had saved went so fast…"

"Lots of people go through hard times, Mom. I still don't understand why you left."

Kate was quiet for a minute.

"Everything just began to unravel, to go wrong. We were struggling and couldn't pay our bills. We lived in crummy houses and trailers. Your dad worked so hard—he took one ranch hand job after another to keep us going. We had to buy your clothes at yard sales."

A painful memory stabbed at Jesse.

"I remember going to those yard sales," he said softly. "In fourth grade, when we were living in Cody, I went to school wearing one of Tyler Hutton's old shirts. He told everyone in the class."

"Oh, Jess."

Kate looked like her heart would break. Jesse had to turn away. He hated to see her sad.

"That must have been awful. It wasn't what we wanted for you. It was the reality of our lives at the time."

"I know, Mom," Jesse said. He looked out at the stream. Water bugs were skimming along its surface. "Even when I was little, I knew that things weren't always the best, but we were all together, and I never heard you guys arguing."

"We never really did. But as bad as arguing can be, at least we would have been talking with each other. Words do hurt, Jesse, but silence can be just as wounding. Your dad and I were like strangers to each after a while."

"You didn't love him anymore?"

"I loved him very much. I still do. That's never been the issue."

"Then tell me what is," Jesse said.

"We weren't kids sneaking out to the rodeo anymore. We were married adults with a child. Neither one of us had a college degree, so our job prospects weren't great. I was very, very unhappy."

"So you left."

"I left." Kate nodded. "We were living at the Garrity Ranch at the time. It was in the middle of nowhere. Endless dust. Tumbleweeds. Empty plains. I couldn't breathe there. That's what it felt like. Suffocating. Every day on the way home from my cashier's job, I wanted to just keep driving when I saw the sign for the ranch. I wanted to escape.

"So, I left and moved to Laramie. I qualified for student aid and enrolled at the University of Wyoming."

Jesse felt tears welling in his eyes. He stood and walked a few feet away as they rolled down his cheeks. Kate came to him and put her arms around him.

"I was young, Jesse, and I didn't think I could make you or your dad happy if I wasn't happy. But it's okay to be mad at me. You have every right to be mad at me."

Jesse swiped at his eyes.

"No, you're my mom, and I love you."

"I wanted to take you with me, but you were so happy at the ranch."

"How do you know I wouldn't have been just as happy in Laramie with you?"

"You were learning to ride. You loved everything about the ranch and everything about horses. I didn't want to take you away from that. You would have had a very different life in the city." She let out a long sigh. "I can't go back and change the decisions I made, Jesse. I can only move forward and learn from my mistakes."

"None of that matters now, Mom. You're back for good. Just bring your stuff over. I'll help you unpack. Just come home."

"Oh, Jesse, I *am* home."

"What does that mean?"

"I'm living in Lander. I've got a great job. I'm saving to get my own place."

"No, Mom, I'm talking about *our* house—mine and Dad's. We'll all live together and be a family again."

"You can see and talk to me whenever you want. All you have to do is call me. And I'll call you a lot, too."

"But you said you loved him."

"I do, Jesse. But I'm not going to live with him again. That's over."

"How do you know? He asked you to come home."

Kate shook her head. "He hasn't asked in a while. Even if he did, I'd say no. We've grown apart. Sometimes it happens, Jess. We were just teenagers when we married."

A jolt of pure shock run through his body. He jumped to his feet.

"*Go!*" he shouted. "I don't want to talk to you anymore. And I don't want to see you anymore right now."

CHAPTER 42

HE TOOK OFF RUNNING AND DIDN'T STOP UNTIL HE REACHED the house. He darted into his bedroom, slammed the door, and dropped onto his bed so hard he bounced. He lay on his back, breathing hard, hot tears stinging the corners of his eyes.

This was not at all what he had expected. He'd always believed that someday his mom would come home. Now everything was messed up, and he didn't know whom to blame—his dad for not wanting his mom to come back, or his mom for starting it all in the first place.

He heard her truck start up. He got up from the bed and went to the window, parted the curtains and peeked out into the yard. Kate's truck was gone.

Good, he thought as fresh tears flooded his eyes, *I'm glad she left. What good does it do for her to tell me she loves me if she isn't coming back?*

Jesse was drinking a Coke in the kitchen when Mark walked in the door a few hours later.

"You're home early."

"Your mom called me a little while ago."

Jesse tossed the empty can into the trash.

"I guess she hates me," he said.

"Do you really believe that?"

Jesse didn't answer. He felt raw—wounded. As worried as he was about Aaron, he couldn't remember a time when he'd felt as sad as he did now.

"Jesse, I still love your mom, but somehow, I think you've gotten the idea that she and I…"

Mark shook his head and turned away. He didn't seem able to find the words he wanted.

Jesse knew, then. His parents were not getting back together. Not now. Not ever. As sad as he felt, he also felt foolish, like a little kid.

"Are you okay, Jesse? I heard you guys had quite a day. Your mom said—"

"I'm tired, Dad." Jesse's anger was spent, but he didn't feel like being around either of his parents. He went to his room and dropped down on his bed again, bouncing right on top of Aaron's large dreamcatcher, the one made with Reuben's silver shirt buttons.

He pulled it out from under his back and held it at arm's length above him. What was it doing on his bed? He hadn't taken it out of his closet. Or had he? He'd been so upset after talking with his mom. Maybe he just didn't remember.

He rolled to his side and shoved the dreamcatcher under his bed. He had too much to deal with all at one time. He kicked off his shoes, lay flat on his back, and closed his eyes, intending to take a short nap before dinner.

Hours later, he opened his eyes to the sound of footsteps outside his window. His room was dark and quiet, and he realized he had slept into the night. He heard the footsteps again and groaned; it better not be Cade out there.

He pushed out of bed and parted the curtains that covered the window.

Dreamcatcher stood outside in the darkness. He was different, wilder looking, as if no one had ever sat on his back. He snorted and shook his head, sending his mane flying in all directions. A tuft of his forelock fell over brown eyes that regarded Jesse with a terrible intensity.

Jesse opened the window and climbed out, his sock-clad feet sliding on the dewy grass.

"Hey, boy," he murmured.

The mustang snorted again, wheeled, and galloped toward the woods. Jesse looked over his shoulder at the house. No time to wake his dad. He left his socks on the ground and took off running.

CHAPTER 43

THE WOODS WERE DENSE, MUCH DENSER THAN HE REMEM-bered. Heavy branches slowed him down, and he lost sight of the mustang. Exhaling loudly, Jesse pushed the last branch aside and stepped not onto the banks of the stream behind his house but into a clearing.

He was back on the mountain, back in the place where he and Cade had found Aaron.

A man sat on the same fallen tree limb Aaron had sat on just a few weeks before. His back was to Jesse, and his head was down. Something was lying in the dirt by his feet. Jesse leaned over the man's shoulder for a closer look. It was Aaron's large dreamcatcher.

"How did you get that?" he demanded. "I just put that under my bed."

The man snatched the dreamcatcher off the ground and shot to his feet. He was tall and muscular, and Jesse instinctively took a few steps back. The man turned slowly to face him.

It was the man in Cade's photograph. The only thing missing was the beaded headband.

The beaded headband in Jesse's pocket.

It *had* been Reuben he'd seen at the gates of Savage Ranch on that very first day. It *had* been Reuben outside his window that night, Reuben who had looked down at him in the gorge and followed him up on the mountain.

But Reuben Little Elk was dead.

Wasn't he?

Jesse backpedaled, but Reuben followed, holding the dreamcatcher out, begging him with his eyes to take it.

"I don't want it back," Jesse yelled as he fled backwards. "I don't even know why Aaron gave it to me."

Reuben came faster, arms still extended, backing Jesse up to the edge of the ravine.

"Okay, okay!" Jesse glanced over his shoulder.

He gently took the dreamcatcher. Reuben dropped his arms. Something dark dripped from his sleeves and pooled at his feet.

No, Jesse pleaded. *No.*

He reached out and opened Reuben's jacket. He saw the red, gaping hole where Reuben's stomach should have been.

Shock silenced his tongue, but it couldn't stop his feet. He staggered back, losing his balance when the ground suddenly disappeared beneath his heels. He plunged head-first into the darkness of the ravine. The scream that had been stuck in his throat only seconds before came roaring out.

The ground rushed up to meet him. He squeezed his eyes shut, anticipating the impact.

Here it comes...

Jesse bolted up in bed. His hair was plastered to his head with the sweat that soaked his body. He sat rigid, arms folded across his chest, sucking air into his lungs.

The room was quiet and dark, the window closed and locked. He slid to the floor and poked his head under the bed. Nothing but a few balled-up socks and a homework assignment he'd have sworn he turned in.

He got up on his knees and rested his forehead against the side of the mattress. He peeked with one eye and saw that the dreamcatcher was now hanging on the wall over his bed.

CHAPTER 44

JESSE WALKED WITH A NURSE THROUGH THE ICU TO AARON'S room. He waited for the her to leave.

Aaron lay still, unmoving, his breathing rhythmic, his thin chest rising and falling. Jesse sighed, reached over, and gave his friend's hand a squeeze.

He left Aaron's room a few minutes later. Going back to the nurses' station, he removed the yellow gown all ICU visitors were required to wear, pulling it off one sleeve at a time and stuffing it in a hamper.

"Visit over already, sweetie?" one of the nurses asked, looking up from a patient chart. "Come back and see him soon, okay?"

"I'm hoping I don't have to come back here to see him," Jesse said.

The nurse smiled. "Do you know something we don't?"

"Not me," he answered. "But I think his brother does."

He left the ICU a few minutes later, shoving his hands into his pockets as he began the long walk down the florescent-lit green-tiled hallway. It was a busy hallway—orderlies pushing carts full of equipment and patients in wheelchairs; family members, some tired-looking and crying, others joyful, carrying flowers, cards, and teddy bears, hunting for the elevators that would take them to their loved ones rooms. Announcements crackled from speakers overhead. A white-haired doctor dressed in pale-blue scrubs smiled as he passed.

But Jesse's mind was on Aaron and the dreamcatcher now hanging above his ICU bed.

CHAPTER 45

THE CALL CAME AT 6 P.M. IT WAS AARON'S ICU NURSE.

"Come to the hospital," she said. "Come now. Come quickly."

That's all she said.

The ride to the hospital was tense and quiet. Jesse and his dad barely spoke to each other. Was whatever had happened so bad the nurse couldn't talk about it on the phone?

Jesse was glad Mark didn't force conversation. He was worried about Aaron, and also still angry with both his parents. Kate had called a couple of times and even stopped over at the house once, but he hadn't said much more than "hello" and "goodbye." He had been spending most of his time with Big Bob and Beau, working around the ranch.

Big Bob found out about Jesse and Cade's exploits at the New Market auction, of course, but he wasn't angry. He drove to New Market to smooth things over with the auction owner and with Mike Hughes, and he came back with a six-year-old gelding for Jesse.

"Just promise not to jump him over any corral fences," he joked.

Big Bob's generosity overwhelmed Jesse. The horse was handsome and spirited; he spent as much time as he could grooming him, turning him out, and mucking his stall. But he couldn't ride him.

Something was missing. He couldn't stand in the middle of a corral on Savage Ranch and not see Aaron sitting on top of one of the fence rails. It just didn't feel right. He hadn't even thought of a name for the gelding yet.

Now something had happened to Aaron in the hospital.

They hurried to the ICU nurses' station together. Dread washed over Jesse when he noticed no one was smiling. He handed a yellow gown to his dad and put one over his own clothes.

He headed to Aaron's room alone, listening to his own footsteps all the way down the hallway. When he got there, he took a deep breath and walked in.

Three doctors, two nurses, and Aaron's parents surrounded the bed.

This is bad, he thought. *Really bad.*

He couldn't see Aaron at all. Tears started to fill his eyes. Something terrible had happened.

He backed up to the door, ready to run to his father. He bumped into an IV pole and sent it clattering to the floor. The noise startled the three doctors, two nurses, and Aaron's parents, who all turned toward the him. Seven pairs of eyes found Jesse.

One of the nurses reached out and took his arm. She pulled him up to Aaron's bedside.

I'm not ready to see this, he wanted to scream. *I'm not ready to see him...*

Propped up in bed eating a Popsicle?

"Jesse!" Aaron greeted him, his voice hoarse from the tubes that had only recently been removed from his nose and throat, "I've got a popsicle! I bet they'll give you one, too. Do you want me to ask?"

Jesse felt lightheaded.

"Wow," he said, "I thought…I thought you were…"

"Were what?" Aaron asked, his lips and mouth stained bright red from the cherry Popsicle, which was dripping over his hand and down onto the bed.

"Asleep," Jesse said. "I thought you were asleep."

"Woke up just after you left," the nurse said. "Just after you hung that pretty dreamcatcher over his bed."

She left then, followed by the doctors and Aaron's parents.

"I had a dream right before I woke up," Aaron said. "The mustang was back with his herd. Back where he should be."

"No one's ever going to catch him again."

"Reuben was there, too. I couldn't see him, but I heard his voice, telling me to wake up, people needed me. Stupid, huh? Who needs *me*?" He finished the last of his Popsicle and laid the stick on the table beside his bed. He wiped his sticky hands across the hospital gown and rested his head back against the pillow. He was tiring already.

"My dad told me everything that happened. I'm sorry you got so sick, Jesse. But your mom's here—right? You must be happy."

"I'm not hanging around her much these days."

"That makes me sad, Jesse. I hope it wasn't my fault. I never thought anyone would ever go looking for me."

"No, it's not your fault. And why would you think no one would look for you. That's crazy."

"It's like I'm invisible until some kid wants someone to pick on. Some teachers only see me when I don't come to school. You're really the only friend I've ever had, Jesse."

"I wasn't the best friend I could be."

"Don't say that. You came after me! And you saved me."

"It wasn't all me. It wasn't even my idea—it was Cade's. Even the mustang did more than I did."

195

"That's not what my dad said."

"Some really weird things happened up in the mountains. Here, too. I know I had help."

A smile flickered across Aaron's face.

"Reuben always says the hardest things to see are the ones right in front of our faces." His smile faded, and the corners of his mouth turned down. "Said. That's what he always said," Aaron whispered.

"I'm sorry about Reuben. "

Aaron looked down and picked at a thread on his hospital gown.

"I know my brother is dead. I know he's never coming back—at least not in the way I want him to. All the dreamcatchers in the world aren't going to change that."

Jesse pulled a chair up.

"Put your hand out." He reached into his pocket and pulled out the red-beaded headband. He placed it into the other boy's outstretched hand.

A tear trickled down Aaron's face as he closed his hand around it.

"Everything is different without him."

"Reuben will always be around for you, Aaron."

"But I'll never hear his voice again." Aaron turned his head to gaze at the peaks of the Wind River out the window. "The mountains will always be empty without him. Who'll take me fishing, Jesse? Who'll teach me about training horses?"

"I've lived on five different ranches, Aaron. You are already a better trainer than a lot of the men I've seen."

"But why didn't Reuben come to me, Jesse? *You* saw him. Cade, too. "

"I think he was protecting you. Letting you know he can't really come back. It's like he was saying you don't have to see him to know he's around. Your whole life can't be about missing Reuben. You gotta let him go a little bit."

Aaron nodded. "It's just me and my mom and dad, now. It's not the family I want, but it's the family I have, and I'm going to be happy. Like you have to be, Jesse."

"What? No, that's different. My mom is here."

Aaron yawned. "What difference does that make if you won't see her? Maybe it's time for you to stop being sad. To let stuff go, too."

The truth of what Aaron had just said hit Jesse. Reuben was right. The hardest things to see are the ones right in front of our faces.

"No more running away to the mountains by yourself, Aaron, okay?"

"I won't, Jesse, I promise." Aaron smiled. "I'll ask Cade to take me."

Jesse laughed. "Deep down, we all know Cade's got a heart of gold."

Aaron rolled his eyes. "I reckon we'll be best friends after I get out of here. Maybe he'll buy me boots from Chandlers for my birthday."

"Yeah? Well, I think Reuben should visit Cade more often, then. Like maybe on my birthday, too. I could use a new pair of boots."

Both boys were laughing now, and the noise brought the nurse back into the room.

"Just a few more minutes, Jesse. Aaron needs his rest."

"Okay," Jesse said. "I won't stay long."

"Thanks." She left with a bright smile.

Jesse watched her out of the room.

"You've sure got some pretty nurses."

Aaron shifted in the bed.

"Did you miss the rodeo because of me. Are you mad?"

"Nope. Besides, Big Bob gave me another horse."

"That's gr—" Aaron stopped, his brow creased in concern. "What breed?"

Jesse laughed. "This one's a quarterhorse, a solid chestnut gelding. And I get to keep him. He's all mine."

"That's great, Jesse. I can't wait to see him. Is he fast? I bet he's a rocket. I bet he could jump the moon."

"Yeah, he's fast—just about finished, too. Still…"

"Still what?" Aaron asked.

"Jesse?" the nurse called.

"I'm leaving."

"Still what?" Aaron was sitting straight up now.

"Gotta go," Jesse said, putting the chair back in its place. "They're kicking me out."

"*Still what?*" Aaron demanded.

"I'm going to need someone to help me bring him along. Someone who understands horses. Someone who can make a connection with them."

Aaron's eyes widened. "Are you talking about me?"

Jesse headed for the door.

"Well, duh," he said.

CHAPTER 46

JESSE LEFT THE HOSPITAL WITH HIS DAD, STEPPING INTO THE warmth of the summer evening. A breeze, sudden, brief, and familiar, rushed to find him. Jesse closed his eyes for a moment and let it envelop him. It carried an unmistakable smell—the smell of the woods of the Wind River Reservation, of the red hard-packed dirt of the canyon…

And of the paint mustang. He couldn't touch it, he couldn't see it, but he could feel it.

He opened his eyes and found his dad staring at him. "You okay, Jess?"

"Yeah, Dad, I am." A smile, the first in many days, broke across his face.

Mark pulled his keys out of his pocket.

"Jess, I called your mom while you were in with Aaron, just to let her know he's okay."

Jesse nodded. Living with his dad while his mom lived across town wasn't the family he wanted, but it was the family he had. Reuben was gone; Aaron would never have his brother back. But Jesse's mom, even if she wasn't in the next room, was still here. He'd just to have to try and deal with it.

"Dad, did you really have to give up your dreams of buying a ranch because of me?"

Mark inserted the key into the ignition. He sat back and studied his son.

"Where did that come from? You must have had some talk with your mom." He leaned toward Jesse and put a hand on his shoulder. "Look at me, Jesse, and listen. You are the best thing that's ever happened to me. There isn't a ranch in the world I'd take over you. I am a lucky man, Jesse, because you are my son."

"But you never did get your ranch. Aren't you even a little disappointed?

"Who says I won't get my own place someday? Big Bob pays well. And I'm only thirty-five years old."

"Well, that's kinda old…"

Mark laughed. "I'm not ready for the rocking chair on the porch yet. The great thing about dreams is, they only die if you let them. Okay? Are we good, now?"

"We're definitely good, Dad."

Jesse leaned out of the pickup's window as they rumbled out of the hospital parking lot. The truck's engine sputtered. Mark rapped on the dashboard.

"C'mon, you can make it! Maybe I better get us a newer truck before I put a down payment on that ranch."

Jesse laughed. Head resting on crossed arms, he peered up at the twilight sky. Stars and a full moon were beginning to emerge. What was it Aaron had said about his new horse and the moon?

"Let's catch the special at the diner tonight," Mark said. "Been a while since we ate out. Then we can head on home."

"Sounds good, Dad.

Aaron would be out of the hospital soon, and the promise of a wide-open summer lay before them. Tonight, though, he and his dad would go to the diner and have the fried chicken special. Then he'd go back to Savage Ranch—to their home—and to a horse named Rocket, who could jump the moon.

END

ABOUT THE AUTHOR

ANN CURTIN was born in Baltimore, Maryland. She received a Bachelor of Arts in Anthropology from the University of Maryland and a Master's in Education from the College of Notre Dame of Maryland. She worked as an archaeologist and is now a middle school history teacher. She lives in Annapolis, Maryland, with her husband Jerry and their two dogs and one cat.

ABOUT THE ARTISTS

EVA MONTEALEGRE's organic spiritual connection is always present as a through-line in her artistic expression. She started as a graphic designer, but the pure act of creating art for its own sake captured her soul and would not let go.

Her gallery debut was at Long Beach Arts gallery, where her mixed-media sculpture, *Lady Starkskull Ponders the Cosmos*, was awarded a prize. Her painting *Moon One* is featured in the art book *Art Takes Times Square*, and her figurative painting of a woman titled *Creative Call* is featured in the art book *Women's Rights: An Artist's Perspective*. She recently received a composer's award for a song she authored related to the theme of her painting *Alligator Woman*.

She is interested in continually exploring the origins of man's humanity through the examination of artwork first created in cave paintings and works on projects that allow for recognizing and affirming the progression of creativity from the first artwork created to today's modern art.

TAMIAN WOOD is currently based in sunny South Florida. Using art, photography, typography and digital collage techniques, she creates book covers that appeal to the eye and the mind, to entice the book browser to become a book reader. She holds degrees in computer science and graphic design and is a proud member of Phi Theta Kappa National Honour Society.